Finding Daddy

Finding Daddy

Louise Plummer

DELACORTE PRESS

Published by Delacorte Press
an imprint of Random House Children's Books
a division of Random House, Inc.
New York

www.randomhouse.com/teens

Educators and librarians, for a variety of teaching tools, visit us at
www.randomhouse.com/teachers

Library of Congress Cataloging-in-Publication Data

Plummer, Louise.
 Finding Daddy / Louise Plummer. — 1st ed.
  p. cm.
 Summary: Just before her sixteenth birthday, Mira finally tracks down the father she has never known, but a few days before meeting him—without her mother's or grandmother's knowledge—someone breaks into their home, beginning an escalating series of crimes.
 ISBN-13: 978-0-385-73092-1 (trade)
 ISBN-13: 978-0-385-90113-0 (glb)
 [1. Fathers and daughters—Fiction. 2. Psychopaths—Fiction. 3. Love—Fiction.
4. Family Life—Utah—Fiction. 5. Utah—Fiction.] I. Title.
PZ7.P734Fin 2007
[Fic]—dc22
                                        2006023938

5162

The text of this book is set in 13-point Garamond #3.

Printed in the United States of America

10 9 8 7 6 5 4 3 2 1

First Edition

In memory of
Lucy Gladys Plummer
April 16, 2004–August 7, 2004

Chapter One

Saturday

I miss my father, a strange thing to say, because I've never known him, never laid eyes on him. My mother and grandmother conspire to keep information about him to themselves. "You have all of his good qualities," Mom says from behind the stack of AP English papers. She is defined by her English-teacher objects: the green desk lamp, her antique reading glasses, the black fountain pen. I don't remember a school night when she wasn't writing in margins with that Waterman pen she received from my grandmother the night I was born. "You have his red hair, his ability to put words together, to draw, to appreciate beauty and silence." The pen is poised at her lips when she turns her head toward the window and the sound of a barking dog. "His seriousness." She turns back and looks at me directly. "Those compelling green eyes." She smiles.

"Except for the looks and the drawing, those sound

like your gifts," I say. I sit against the sofa arm, my head resting on my raised knees.

"You think?" She pushes a strand of hair away from her eyes and returns to the papers. The hair falls back. She is growing it out and it will not stay put. My father's bad qualities seem suspended in the air between us. It is no use asking about them again. She will not tell, nor will my grandmother, who says, "He always loved my Belgian waffles."

So does the dog.

My mother says, "He's not someone we want in our lives," and leaves it at that. I was never part of that decision.

Once, in a moment when I had worn her down, she told me his first name: Ambrose. Not his last. Her name is the same as her mother's: Kent. As in Clark Kent. Only she is Charlotte Kent. My grandmother is Mirabella Kent (I call her Bella) and I am Mira. We are a matriarchal household. No basso profundos bellowing here. Our tensions are strictly female and since the three of us are "amiable"—I like that Jane Austen word—there is little conflict. It's boring.

So I miss my father the same way I miss a howling wind that forces a placid ocean into crushing waves, even though I've never seen it. I miss him like tiramasu and escargot and all the other exotic-sounding foods I've never eaten. What can I say? I just miss him.

Bella lets the caramel syrup drip from an oversized wooden spoon onto the Belgian waffles. As long as I can remember, she has fixed Belgian waffles on Saturday mornings, accompanied by berries, syrup (often chocolate), and whipped cream. She wears a Williams-Sonoma apron over a designer pantsuit, because she always has a couple of open houses on Saturday. She is a trillion-dollar real estate broker—Mirabella Kent and Associates. Her signs are posted in front of pricey homes all over the city. It's because of her that we live in upscale Federal Heights, an old tree-lined neighborhood in Salt Lake City.

My two best friends, Sarah Sullivan and Dylan Madsen—actually, he's my boyfriend now—and I are sitting at the kitchen table in our pajamas. This is an old tradition that goes back to seventh grade. They both live on the block and come over each Saturday still wearing their jammies. We brush our teeth but we don't fix our hair, so we look like a family. Bedraggled. I think Bella made up that rule. Now that Dylan and I are together I feel a little self-conscious looking so sloppy in front of him. Maude, our dog—think conventional fluffy white ball—begs at Bella's feet for bacon.

"Has anyone let Maude out this morning?" Bella asks.

"Not me," I say.

"She's probably peed in your office," Sarah wisecracks. "Twice."

"I let her out when I got here," Dylan says.

"You're too sexy for your shoes." Bella smooches the air in Dylan's direction and he blushes. I blush a sympathy blush. She drops a bit of bacon for the dog. "That's it!" She shakes an index finger at the dog. As if.

"You're the sexy one," Dylan says, going on the offensive with Bella. "I have to take a cold shower when I leave this place. Can't stop thinking of you."

Bella doesn't turn her head. "I know that," she spits out. "You've had the hots for me for years."

Sarah heehaws. "It's love. L-O-V-E." She mimes the spelling across the table. "Everyone's in love." She flutters her eyelashes at Dylan and me.

"Give me a break," Dylan says.

I kick her foot under the table.

"Okay, we've got a stack here." Bella turns with a plate of waffles. "This one's for you, Sarah Smartass," Bella says.

Sarah ogles the waffles and the choice of toppings and gushes, "I want you to adopt me. I'll even be your slave. Please, Bella. I'll do the paperwork."

Bella's laugh is low and sultry. At sixty-five, she really is the sexiest woman in our house. "There's no need to adopt you," she says. "You're here almost every day as it is. If you lived here officially you'd get bossed around. Ask Mira."

"You would," I said. "She's a witch."

"She is the angel of waffles," Dylan says. Bella has loaded his plate.

"Kiss-up," I say. He gives me the cutest look. I still can't believe we're actually a couple.

Bella sets a plate of waffles down in front of me. "There you go, *Red*." A reference to my hair.

"Witch!" I say.

"Red, Red, Red."

"Witch, Witch, Witch!" It's an old game and we both smirk.

With her mouth full, Sarah says, "See, now that's why I want you to adopt me. My mother never lets us joke around like that. She'd say, 'Stop calling each other names.'" She swallows. "No sense of humor."

"She's got to have a sense of humor living in your house. Your dad is the funniest guy I know," I say.

"My mother doesn't think so. She thinks he's a dork."

Dylan's lips form an *O*. "Oh, let's put that through the neighborhood rumor mill."

Sarah shrugs. "It's no secret. She's always saying she thought she married a thoracic surgeon, not Red Skelton."

"Who's Red Skelton?" I ask.

Bella releases a loud *ha*. She pries a waffle loose from the iron and onto a plate. "Your parents are both lovely people," she says, a half smile on her lips. We watch her swirl the caramel sauce with the wooden spoon. She is an artist. She spoons strawberries and cream onto the top and sets the plate on a tray. "Otherwise"—she leans her face up close to Sarah's—"they wouldn't have such a wonderful daughter—a daughter I would gladly adopt as my own." She swivels around, picks up the tray, and heads into the hallway. The dog follows her. "I'm taking this up to Charlotte," she says.

"The house is full of kiss-ups this morning," I yell after her.

"You could learn something from us," she yells back.

"Who is Red Skelton?" I ask Sarah, but before she can answer, the clock in the hall dings the half hour and Dylan is on his feet. "I've gotta go. I have to help my father paint my grandma's garage and I told him I'd be ready at eight-thirty, sharp." He takes his food with him. "I'll return the plate!" he yells, and he's out the front door. Then the door opens, and he calls, "You guys want a ride to the yearbook signing party tonight?"

Sarah and I yell yes in unison.

"Meet me out in front at seven," he calls, and the door shuts again. My mood falls a little with his sudden departure. I was hoping we could laze around this morning.

"Okay," I say to Sarah. "Now, who is Red Skelton?"

Her shoulders slump and she makes a face that says *Duh*. "Do I have to teach you everything about American popular culture?" She talks with her mouth full, which I will never get used to.

"Just tell me, okay? I don't need a lecture."

"Do you even know who Chubby Checker is?"

"Is it important?"

Her eyes roll heavenward. "Red Skelton is a comic from the fifties—he had a very popular television show called *The*—" She waits for me to finish.

I play along. *"The Red Skelton Show?"*

"Very good." Really, sometimes I'd like to punch her. "Anyway, he wore goofy clothes, talked with a lisp, and did a lot of fall-down stuff. My dad has all the DVDs of him, and my mom can't stand the guy." She sips orange juice. "He had red hair about the same color as yours."

I sit up then. "Maybe he's my father!" I say.

Sarah rolls her eyes. "Obsessive. It's all you talk about lately. You have a father fixation." Her eyes bug out at me.

I lower my voice. "Well, no one in this house will tell me anything about him."

"You have a picture of him in your room."

"What can I tell from a picture?" I lick whipped cream from my spoon. "They were divorced when I was three. Why did they divorce? Why are Mom and Bella so uncommonly sweet about him and so vague at the same time? Wouldn't that drive you mad?"

"I guess." She pulls a scrunchie out of her pocket and gathers her hair back. "But you never seemed worried about it before."

"I know. I guess I've just been wondering about it more lately, and when I ask a question, they're so mysterious it makes me curious. I don't even know his last name. Why can't they tell me his name?"

She leans forward and says in a stage whisper, "Maybe he's a criminal."

I nod. "I've thought of that."

Her dark hair is back in a ponytail now. "What about your birth certificate?"

"What about it?"

"His name would be on your birth certificate."

My jaw drops. "It would—"

"Duh—mine's in my baby book. Mom made a pocket for it, so it can come out when I need it—oh, oh, oh—" She bobs up and down. "You need it when you get your learner's permit! I remember. You need to show your birth certificate!" Sarah clasps her hands. "That's only a month away."

"June eighteenth," I breathe. "June eighteenth and I will see my father's full name." I hear Bella's footsteps on the stairs. "Shhh," I say. "I mean it, shush."

"I can keep your dirty little secret," Sarah scoffs.

"Was Mom up?" I ask when Bella returns.

"She is now. Eating like a lioness." She looks at Dylan's empty seat. "Where's my lover boy?"

"He had to help his father," I say. "He took the plate with him."

She smiles. "Love me, love my waffles," she says. "Do you girls want more? I have plenty of batter."

Sarah shoves her chair back. "No, thanks, I've got to go home or Mom will throw a hissy fit." She busses her dishes to the sink. "Thank you, darling Bella, as always." She kisses the air.

Bella kisses the air in return. "G'bye, Sarah Bear."

I walk Sarah to the front door. "See ya."

"I'm babysitting Josh today. Come over if you want."

I nod and watch her run down the street toward her house, which has a mother and a father and an eight-year-old brother. So normal. I sigh. I know I'm feeling sorry for myself and have no reason. I love Bella, and Mom. I love this street lined with mature budding sycamore trees and this big old redbrick house with the black shutters and the heavy brass knocker on the front door. It's the only house I've ever known. I love spring with the late tulips bursting into bloom next to the waxy green leaves of the euonymus bushes. I love the stretch of yellow roses along the side of the house. I should be grateful. I sit down on the front step. The smell of lilacs wafts through the air. Dylan backs out of the driveway in his dad's pickup and gives the horn a short toot. I smile back. His father waves. I hug my knees and call through the open front door to Bella: "I'll do the dishes."

"I know you will, Red," she calls back. "I've got to get going."

It's not like I haven't had a father figure in my life. Dr. Sullivan used to take both Sarah and me to the daddy/daughter parties at the church when we were young, and I've been to their cabin on Bear Lake a jillion times. Dr. Sullivan taught me how to water-ski and how to fix a flat on my bike. He taught me to play tennis and how to do push-ups. And he's stitched me up a couple of times, once when I split my knee after falling from my bike and another time when Sarah and I were wrestling and I cut a gash into my arm at the edge of their Ping-Pong table. He's even yelled at me a couple of times, like when I took the kayak out on the lake without wearing a life jacket. He about had a cow. Sarah said he was shouting at me from shore, but I was too far out to hear him. When I did get within hearing distance, I really got an earful. Swearing and all.

Dr. Sullivan is *like* a father to me, but he *isn't* my father. Big difference.

"Oh, you're out here—" Mom is in the doorway wearing her Old Navy sweats and holding Maude in her arms.

I turn. "I was just saying good-bye to Sarah, and spring caught me by surprise," I say. "It's a beautiful day."

She hovers in the doorway, looking up and down the street, her hand stroking Maude's head. "It's a perfect day," she says, and sits on the step next to me. "I thought I'd go shopping at Gateway. Want to go?"

"Sounds fun," I say, "but I told Sarah I'd come over and help her take care of Josh." I'm surprised by my easy lie. "He minds me better than her."

A half smile, half nod from Mom. She puts Maude down on the sidewalk and the dog lies in our shade, her head resting on her paws.

We turn when the garage door opens. Maude growls. Bella in her Mercedes backs out into the driveway. The driver's side window is open. "I'll be at the Openshaw house over on Wolcott until one and then that monstrosity out on Cottonwood from two to four. You want to go for Chinese tonight?"

"Great!" I say. Mom nods and waves.

"Toodleoo, then." She kisses the air and backs recklessly out of the driveway.

"Is she wild or what?" I say.

Mom laughs. "You should have seen her and Daddy together. They were a real pair." She pauses. "I wish you could have known him."

For a second I think she means *my* dad, but before I say anything I realize she is talking about her own father, who died suddenly when she was in college.

"You still think about him?" I ask.

"The longer he's gone the more I miss him," she says. "I had great parents and took it for granted that everyone in the world was like them. Then . . ." Her voice falters.

I know what the unfinished sentence is: *Then I married your father.*

"Didn't he work for Grandpa and Bella?" I already know the answer, but I like to get her to talk about him. Maybe something new will slip out.

"He was a real estate genius—their best salesman by far. He made a good living even during the recession." She brushes her hair back from her eyes. "I never had to worry about money with him."

I hear the implied idea that there were plenty of other things to worry about. I put my arm through hers and look into her face. "Well, what was it *exactly*? I mean, why—"

She covers my hand with her own, but her face shows exasperation. "What is all this new interest in your father? I've told you when we separated we decided that he would not be a part of your life. It was planned, Mira. Some people shouldn't be parents. I have no idea where he is now. I don't want to know."

"I don't care if he's not the perfect dad type. I just want to know who he is. He wouldn't mind—now that I'm almost sixteen—if I wanted to look him up—"

"No!" She breaks loose and stands up. "No, Mira. No. That's final." She disappears inside the front door.

I follow. "That's final? How can it be final? I'm here because of the two of you. Didn't you think I would grow up and ask questions?"

"Well, it *is* final." She circles the kitchen table as if she wants to cut a path through the hardwood floor. "Please, Mira, just leave it alone. Please."

I've never seen my mother this upset, and it scares me. "Was he some kind of deviant?" My voice has lost its punch. "Was he a serial killer? Did he like young boys or something? Was he, you know, like Hannibal Lecter? Tell me. I can take it." When I step toward her she backs away from me, her pressed lips distorted with emotion.

"It isn't that easy," she whispers. "Please don't press me on this." She's into the hallway and up the stairs. "I'm getting dressed," she says.

"What about grandparents?" I call after her. "Do I have other grandparents besides Bella?" No answer.

I think her secretiveness is wrong. I think I have a

right to know my own father and his side of the family. And I'm not waiting until my birthday, because I know that Mom will find a way to keep the birth certificate out of my view.

I'll just have to find it myself before then.

Chapter Two

I stay out of Mom's way until I hear the garage door open
and close, then look out my bedroom window to see her
Honda disappear down the street. "Come on, Maudie," I
say to the dog. "Let's go solve a mystery." Maude yips
around my feet, probably hoping we're going for a
walk. When I turn away from the front door at the bottom of the stairs, she lets out a bark. "This way," I call
back to her.

Mom and Bella each have a study on the first floor.
Bella has the "library"—her real estate term—with the
cherry bookcases lining the walls. Mom's study is really a
garden room off the kitchen. It's all windows and looks
out over the backyard. Her desk sits out in the middle of
the room. There's a sofa on the only wall, which is where
I like to sit and read. All of Mom's books—and there are
hundreds of them—are stacked against the windows and
around her desk. I head toward the two file cabinets at

the far end of the room. I feel dumb because I never thought to look here for information.

Maude barks at me.

"No!" I shout.

She jumps on the sofa, hunkers down, and follows my movements with her pleading doggy eyes.

Most of the files are lesson plans for classes Mom has taught: *Oedipus; Beowulf; Canterbury Tales;* Shakespeare's sonnets, plays, biography; the Globe Theater; *Pride and Prejudice*; and on and on. The bottom drawer is labeled "taxes." I don't expect to find something as easy as a marker that says "birth certificates." I figure it'll be hidden within another file, but the files labeled taxes are what they say they are. Boring.

I try her desk drawers. There's an old cigar box with photos from long ago: Bella with Grandpa—a striking couple. Mom with them. Mom with college friends. Mom in the convertible she used to drive. Pictures of me growing up. I've seen all these before. I go through the rest of her drawers. No birth certificates. I go back to the file cabinet and browse through the literature files to see if anything is hidden in the folders. I pull the files out and look underneath them. Nothing.

When Maude barks again, I let her out the back door and stand on the patio waiting for her to do her business. She sits on the lawn and stares at me.

"Pee!" I say.

The phone rings and I leave her there while I answer it. "Hello."

"I was just thinking," Sarah begins in mid-thought. "You have to have a birth certificate when you begin school. You have to have one to get your first driver's license. You also need one to get a passport."

"What's your point?"

"Well, what do people do who have lost a birth certificate? I mean, the human race being what it is and everything—you'd think there are bound to be gazillions of people who lose the darn thing. Then what?"

"You're a genius."

"Actually, I really am. My IQ is—"

"You send in for a copy, of course. Why didn't I think of it?"

"Because you're only gifted—"

"Or I could go down to the city and county building on Monday and get a copy. Ohmygosh. Ohmygosh. Ohmygosh." I'm dancing on my toes.

"Exactly. I'll go with you." Her hand muffles the phone. "Josh!" she yells. "Gotta go," she says to me. "I think he's sniffing glue." She hangs up.

I could stop looking, but I feel restless and Monday is a day and a half away. Maude barks at the back door, and I let her in. She follows me into Bella's library. I feel sneaky. I don't hang about Bella's office much. When she's in there, she's busy. You can hear her talking on the phone, and sometimes clients come at night when they're eager to make an offer on a house. Unlike Mom's study, Bella's is neat. Books are shelved according to size. Her desk and credenza are cleared of clutter. Pillows on the sofa are plumped just so. I have the feeling that Bella knows precisely where every bit of paper is located.

Maude jumps on the sofa and nestles into one of the pillows. "Get down!" I yell. I grab her, set her down outside the door, and close it. She whines and paws at the door. "Stop it, Maude!" As if she obeys orders.

The desk isn't locked. Opening a drawer at a time, I carefully lift papers and files to look underneath. Nothing but business. The credenza contains more files, but nothing private.

It's in a bottom drawer of an antique chest that I hit pay dirt. Underneath boxes of brass door knockers—Bella gives them as gifts to clients who have closed on a house—there is a shiny mahogany box with mother-of-pearl flower inlays on the lid. I've never seen this box and rub the top with my fingers. The design is so beautiful that I think it might be a music box, but when I lift the lid there are two family albums. One is larger than the other and is bound in leather. The other album is a perfect square, handmade from thick rippled paper with rough, torn edges. Its cover is painted in watercolor: a red-headed toddler chasing a butterfly. Beneath that in a sure and elegant cursive it reads "Daddy's Little Girl."

I can hardly breathe as I lift it out. Sitting cross-legged on the floor, the book in my lap, I touch the cover with trembling fingertips. "Daddy," I whisper. I know the watercolor is his. Mom has no drawing or painting skills, but I do. I got it from him. She told me that. I got it from Daddy.

The pages are stiff, and I try not to bend them. Each page has a photo of me with my dad. I am very young in the early pictures and then age a little. Sometimes he holds me in his arms, his hair the same burnt red as mine, his smile disarming. I have always had a single framed photo of Daddy in my bedroom but it is different seeing him here. He's laughing and playing with me. These shots are relaxed. He's having fun with his baby daughter. I am sitting on his shoulders, fat hands tugging his hair. The margins are filled with whimsical paintings of flowers, butterflies, and rabbits. The captions in the same neat printing under each photo: "Mira at six months." "Mira on top of the world." "Dad and his girl." Seeing Daddy and me together fills me with longing and loss. Why didn't he want to be with me?

I laugh when I see the last page—I am two or more and have my arm wrapped in a pink cast. I'm sitting on his lap, wailing—it's a real tantrum—back arched, as if struggling to loosen his grip. Underneath is written "Daddy will never let anyone take his girl away from him."

Evidently he was wrong. I start to cry. Why did he change his mind? How could anyone make such a beautiful book for his daughter and then agree to live his life apart from her? It's after I've leafed through the album a dozen times that I realize that my mother isn't in any of the pictures.

Maybe it's a thematic album: Daddy's girl. Maybe there's a companion album: Mommy's girl.

I search in the wooden box but there is only the

leather album. When I turn it over there are gold letters embossed on the left-hand corner: "The Chadwick Family Album."

Who are the Chadwicks?

At the same time I ask the question, I know the answer. Chadwick is Daddy's last name. Ambrose Chadwick. I'm about to open the album when Maude starts up a tremendous barking that alerts me that someone is coming. Seconds later, the garage door opens. It must be Mom.

I put the lid on the box and fit it into the cabinet with the rest of the boxes, grab both albums, and scurry up the stairs to my bedroom, where I hide the albums in my backpack. Then I turn on the shower and get undressed. I don't want to see Mom right now. I don't trust my body. My face burns and my hands tremble. She'll know something is up. I hear her shush the dog and then call my name. I step into the hot jet of water and shut the door behind me. The water beats on me, drumming out the tension. I am safe with my new information for a few minutes. I can hear nothing but my own thoughts: I know who my father is. I know who he is. Ambrose Chadwick. Chadwick. I am Mira Chadwick. Mira Kent Chadwick. I am Ambrose's daughter. Ambrose, who will never let anyone take his little girl away from him.

Mom is at the bottom of the stairs when I finally go down. Seeing the backpack on my shoulder, she says, "You running away from home?" An attempt at humor.

"Yeah, my mother abuses me." I'm standing on the last step looking down at her.

Her smile is pained. "It must seem like it to you." Her hand is at her throat as if it might be closing. "I came back to apologize. I haven't told you everything."

"You haven't told me anything."

She looks away and then into my eyes. "It's not that I don't think you can take the truth about your father and me—" She swallows. "It's that I'm not ready to speak it aloud." She touches my hand, which rests on the finial. "It's me, Mira. It's not you. I'll tell you when I'm ready."

"Okay," I say, although it isn't. "I won't bug you about it for a while." I can be magnanimous with my book bag full of new information.

She smiles then. "And I'll have to think about how to tell you."

"Maybe a letter?" I suggest. "Or a short story?"

"More likely in an epic poem!" Her energy is returning.

"Oh, geez, not epic poetry. I don't want to read any more epic poetry."

"Well, I'll find a shorter genre, then, but I will try." She looks earnest. "I promise."

I don't know what to say, since I'm keeping secrets myself, so I nod. "Okay." She looks like she wants to hug me, but I walk past her. "I'll be at Sarah's if you need me."

Maude is at my heels when I open the front door, eager to follow me out.

Mom picks her up. "Escape while you can," she says.

I can hear Maude barking long after the door is shut.

"I found stuff!" I say to Sarah when she opens the front door. I hold up my backpack.

"The birth certificate?"

"Not quite. I found two albums, though."

She grins. "You've been a busy girl."

I follow her into the living room, where we both plop into a sofa. I start unzipping the backpack and stop. "Where's Josh?" I ask.

"He's eating pizza and doing a puzzle and watching *Shrek* for the zillionth time. He's good for about ten minutes." She rubs her hands together. "Show me what you've got."

I am pathetically grateful for her enthusiasm and I unzip the backpack. She is as impressed with the homemade baby album as I was. "This is gorgeous," she says, and "Look, how cute." She turns the pages slowly. "I can't imagine my dad making a book like this." Is there a tinge of envy in her voice? "Why wouldn't your mother show this to you?" she murmurs. "It's so beautiful." She rubs her fingertips along the edge of the paper. "This is handmade paper." There's respect in her voice.

"You think?"

"I'm sure." She turns a page. "Your dad is really handsome. Too bad you didn't get any of his looks." The edges of her lips curl up.

"Ha, ha, ha—funny girl."

"Ha yourself." She's smiling at the photos. She turns to the last page, where I'm throwing a tantrum.

"Isn't that a riot?" My laugh comes out in a half snort.

Sarah's smile is gone. She reads the caption aloud: "Daddy will never let anyone take his girl away from him." She winces. "Why would he write that?"

"Well, it fits the picture, don't you think? I mean, look how I'm struggling against him." Her serious expression unnerves me a little. "What?" I ask.

"It should say 'Daddy will never let his little girl get away from him.' " She leafs back a few pages and then returns to the last one. "This page is different. The caption is so much longer than any of the others, and *he's* different." She sounds as if she's talking to herself. "His smile—" She's reluctant to describe it. "It's not a smile, really—it's fake."

I move in closer to have a better look. "That's because he's trying to hold down a screaming two-year-old." What is her problem? "It's hard to smile when you've got a—"

"Look at the little cast on your arm." She closes the album and forces a smile. "Sure, you're right," she says, but she's not convincing.

I try again. "That photo bothers you—"

"No." Her arms are folded against her body in a protective posture.

"Why?"

Check Out Receipt

Clifton Park-Halfmoon Public Library (CPH)
518-371-8622

Saturday, April 28, 2012 1:16:21 PM

60263

Item: 0000603045162
Title: Finding daddy
Material: Book
Due: 5/26/2012

Clifton Park-Halfmoon Public Library
Your Community Center for Lifelong Learning

She shifts back into the corner of the sofa, raises her knees into a cross-legged position, and makes fish movements with her closed lips.

I'm supposed to wait when she does this. It means she's thinking, but I can't stand it. "What?" I squeal.

"Remember the last day of sixth grade?"

I groan. "I feel an analogy coming."

"Remember we were dressed up for the graduation program for our families and the rest of the school—"

I let out a snort. "We wore sequins!" Sarah and I had new pastel Gap T-shirts with sparkly stars on the fronts.

Sarah nods. "And we were sitting on bleachers on the stage—I was at the very end—and Miss Gwilliam rehearsed us and then parents started coming into the auditorium and she told us just to sit quietly, only—"

"She had blue teeth!" I throw in. "I was always afraid of gagging when she smiled."

Sarah grabs my leg, which means I should shut up while she finishes the story. "Rocky Gonzales brought his Polaroid." She raises her eyebrows, expecting me to remember something. "And Eugene Detweiler—"

Eugene's name sparks a complete image: "He had a squirt gun that looked like a camera and he filled it with red ink and—ohmygosh!" I cover my mouth with my hands. "Eugene Detweiler was such a hairball."

"Eugene"—Sarah lowers her voice—"squirted me all over my new shirt, my face, my hair, while pretending to take my picture. I fell off the bleachers trying to get away from him and then while I was down, he grabbed me around the neck in a headlock while Rocky 'the creep' Gonzales snapped a real picture." Sarah sneers at the thought of Eugene and Rocky.

"Which he passed to all the boys," I finish. I almost forget why Sarah is telling this story. Sunlight from the windows that face the street emphasizes a smudge along the side of the grand piano. I look down at the book my father—my daddy—made and open it to the last page. "So what are you saying?"

"I don't know exactly." Her fingers twist her hair. "Except that *that* photo reminds me of Eugene Detweiler holding me in a headlock."

"Sarah!"

"Well, you asked!"

"But this is completely different," I say. "It's just a kid having a tantrum. My mom probably shot it thinking it was funny."

She shrugs. "Maybe." She doesn't want to fight with me.

"Really, that doesn't make any sense." I know I sound defensive, but it's important that she see it correctly. She's such a cynic. "I mean, look at the rest of the photos and all the work that's gone into this." I hold up the album. "How can that compare with Rocky Gonzales and Eugene Detweiler? They were a couple of lowlifes. I don't even think they made it into high school."

Sarah holds up the palms of her hands. "Wait," she says. "I just had this reaction about one photo and it reminded me of this thing that happened in sixth grade.

That's all I'm saying." She takes a deep breath. "It probably says more about me than it does about him." She stands up. "I'm going to check on Josh. You want anything from the fridge?"

"Juice."

She disappears through the dining room.

Once more I look at the last page of the album. I don't see what Sarah sees. Silly. I stick it carefully back into my backpack and pull out the the Chadwick family album. It is one of those old albums with a thin layer of vellum between each two pages of photographs. The first page stops my breath. It is a picture of Bella and my grandfather on their wedding day. Bella has the same photo, framed, in her bedroom.

The caption makes my head swirl: "Mr. and Mrs. William Chadwick."

Chapter Three

Chadwick is not my father's name; it's my mother's name. It's Bella's married name. And according to her wedding announcement in the paper, her maiden name was Bateman. Why are we now Kent? It's some kind of mistake, and yet here is my mother as a girl in her bathing suit with a swimming certificate pasted beneath it, issued to Charlotte Chadwick of Roanoke, Virginia. Except as a place on a map, I have never heard of Roanoke, Virginia. Never heard it spoken.

There's a pressure building between my eyes and I press it with the palm of my hand.

"Are you okay?"

I flinch at the sound of Sarah's voice. "Yeah."

She hands me a glass of cranberry juice, and I hold it in my lap. Nothing looks familiar.

"There is too something wrong." Sarah scowls. She sets the juice bottle on the coffee table.

I hand her the Chadwick album. Let her figure it out. She's the genius. I can't put my new knowledge into words yet. Can't speak it aloud.

Sarah sits next to me turning album pages. "What is *this*?"

I stare at the floor, clutching the cold glass of juice.

"Your mom graduated from some girls' academy in Roanoke, Virginia," she says.

"Did she?" I feel heavy.

"I thought she grew up in Kaysville!"

"Me too," I say. What do I know? I obviously don't know anything.

"Ohmygosh!" She grabs my arm. "This is incredible!"

Juice spills onto my jeans. I rub it in.

She sets the album in my lap and, holding it open to a page near the end, says, "It's a copy of your parents' marriage certificate!"

I look down at the two names of the betrothed: Charlotte Louise Chadwick and Paul Earl Weissmann. Across the page is the only photo I've ever seen of my mother and father together. They are in wedding clothes, my mother holding a bouquet of white roses and ivy, and they look radiantly happy.

The only thing I can think to say is "She didn't even tell me his real first name. She can't even say his first name!" I set the glass of juice on the end table and get up and pace. "She and Bella have been lying to me all my life. My whole life is a lie." I smack the side of a fist down on the bass keys of the piano. It makes a satisfying, discordant bong.

"I'm glad my mother isn't here." Sarah grimaces and her eyes bug out a little.

Josh comes running into the living room. "What was that?" he asks. He holds a *Star Wars* action figure and is still wearing his pajamas.

"Nothing," Sarah says. "Mira was practicing the piano."

"She stinks at it." His look challenges me.

"I need lessons." I shoot him a fake smile.

"Josh, if you'll go get dressed, I'll make you a banana split. How about that?" Sarah offers.

He holds his head at an angle while he considers. "Okay!" he yells, and runs off.

"He has the attention span of a chigger," Sarah whispers.

I sit at the piano slumped over in self-pity.

"What are you going to do now?" she asks, sitting next to me on the bench.

I shrug. "I feel like a character in a novel. Some controlling author is putting obstacles in my way."

"It's *The Truman Show*." Sarah nudges me. "I'm an actress playing your best friend. How do you like me so far?"

"If you start speaking in advertisements, I'll know it's true," I say.

"Would you like some more *Ocean Spray Cranberry*?" Both hands point toward the coffee table.

I laugh then and look up at the ceiling for invisible cameras. "Let me out of here," I cry, shaking both fists.

Sarah grins. "This afternoon we've got to think of a plan. Follow me to the war room."

If Sarah's bedroom is the war room, then Sarah is definitely the general. She sits at her desk, spiral notebook open in front of her, and draws a line down the middle of the page. She writes "Options" at the top. Pros on one side and cons on the other. Her first suggestion is that I confront my mother and grandmother and tell them what I know.

I object. I lie spread-eagled on her bed.

Is it vanity, she wants to know.

I don't care what it is, I object.

She says there might be good reasons for their deception.

Like what, I want to know.

Like he's abusive. He's a terrorist. An Iraqi spy. Or on the other hand, he's in the witness protection program, or what makes even more sense, my mother and Bella are in the witness protection program. They witnessed a heinous crime. They witnessed my father committing a heinous crime. Or he comes from a dangerous crime family who are all now spending hard time in a federal penitentiary because of Mom and Bella. Lots of good reasons for their lies. They're protecting me.

I don't buy it. A man who watercolors cannot be abusive. This, I believe, is a cosmic law.

Sarah continues the interview. What do I want? Vengeance? Pure knowledge? Daddy to kiss it better? A movie made for TV? An after-school special? She actually writes all this down.

"I just want to meet him. I don't want to bother Mom and Bella about it. They obviously never want to see him again. Couldn't I meet him without them even knowing? If I could get in touch with him, I could ask him. If he doesn't want to, then that's that. But if he does, then we could arrange a meeting, I'll bet."

Sarah is skeptical. "We don't know where he is. We only have his name."

I snap my fingers. "We'll Google him—you know, a person search."

"Bingo," Sarah says.

But first we have to make Josh a banana split. In the kitchen, Sarah scoops ice cream while I sit tapping the bar underneath my stool with a nervous foot. She makes a chocolate sundae with bananas and gives it to Josh, who returns to the TV, chocolate syrup dribbling down his chin.

Sarah eats straight out of the ice cream carton and hands me a spoon. I join in.

"Josh, you forgot to put your shoes on," she says to him.

He looks up. "I'm going to tell Mom that Mira bonked the piano hard," he says. "She's gonna be mad. She'll choke you like this." He chokes himself with both hands.

"I'm going to choke you, you little bum," I say.

"You said a bad word!" Josh yells. "*Bum* is a bad word."

"I love it when you two talk like brother and sister,"

Sarah says. She motions me to follow her and we go into the den and turn on the computer.

Starting with Google, we use various search engines for Paul Earl Weissmann and come up with zip.

"Maybe we should do one of these paid searches." I point to the screen. "Just thirty bucks and see what they come up with." I feel desperate.

"We know someone who can do what they do. They just search engines we don't have access to." She's biting her lip. When she turns to face me, her look is coy. "I know someone whose father works for a federal agency."

I jump up. "Oh no. *No way*. We are not going there. I'd rather pay the thirty dollars." I pace in a circle. "We're not bringing Dylan into this."

Sarah swivels in her seat. "Why not? He already knows you want to find your dad. This is not news for him. You've been talking about it ever since the Father/Daughter Luau at school."

I shrug. "I'm tired of borrowing your father when I need one."

"I think he likes it," Sarah says.

"Besides, it'd be a felony if Dylan used a federal agency for— He'd need a password. His dad would never let him make that kind of search."

"You don't have to say anything about using the agency—just ask him to help you with the search." Sarah is manipulative, and I tell her so. She shrugs. "Just see what he comes up with."

"You're asking me to set him up. I won't do that to Dylan." I plop back into the leather chair.

Sarah sneers. "Oh puleeze! Since when?"

"Since forever." I shove her chair with my foot.

"Since the Spring Fling." Her voice grows dramatic: "Since the two of you discovered *undying* love for each other." The back of her hand rests against her forehead. "The nobility of it." Her other hand is over her heart. *"I won't do that to Dylan."* She flutters her eyes. Her mimicry of my voice is cruelly exact. I feel silly now. "I'm out of here," I say. I hurry through the hall to the front door. "I'll see you later. I have to go home." I'd like to slam the door, but it's too heavy. I run down the slope of lawn.

Sarah's voice calls after me. "Are you mad? You're not really mad, are you?"

I don't answer but wave with the back of my hand. Sarah can be a bum too. Like brother, like sister. I can't take Sarah's mimicking me. I'm her best friend, and I don't like her making fun of me. Especially Dylan and me. Well, especially me.

The phone is ringing when I open the door. I know it's Sarah and I'm tempted not to answer, but then I do.

"Okay, I suck, I admit it. I won't tease you anymore. Pinky promise."

I smile. "Really?"

"Really. You left your backpack here. Want me to bring it over?"

I catch my breath. I can't be this careless about those

albums. "Put it in your closet, I'll get it tonight." After I promise that I'm really not mad at her, we hang up.

Mom's not home, so I sit at her computer and try the searches again with the same result: nix.

At P. F. Chang's, over dinner, I tell Mom and Bella that I'm going to the yearbook signing party with Dylan and Sarah.

"Sounds fun," Mom says. She's trying to pick up a dumpling with chopsticks and it slips away from her.

"I'd like to see your yearbook sometime," I say to her. "What did you look like at the end of sophomore year in high school?" What I really want to ask is where she went to high school. It certainly wasn't Kaysville.

"Big hair!" She gestures with her hands. "Really big hair. Ghastly."

"I'd like to see it," I say. "I don't think I've ever seen your yearbooks. Are they in your study?" It's an evil question.

"I think they're in storage somewhere. I haven't seen them in years."

"I'll look in my office. They might be in there," Bella says without so much as a flinch.

Mom smiles at her. What a pair. I hardly know who they are. And then it hits me. Maybe they kidnapped me from my father. Parents kidnap kids from each other all the time. I could be one of those kids whose faces appear on milk cartons. I read a novel like that once about a girl who finds her own face on a milk carton. Maybe that's me. I just haven't found the right milk carton yet. This new idea makes me so nervous that I can't eat anymore.

"Aren't you going to eat the rest of your lettuce wraps?" Mom asks.

I shake my head. "I'm full," I say.

"You've barely eaten," Bella says.

"Let me just sit and then I'll try again." I gulp down water to show I'm making an effort.

I decide to talk to Dylan.

Chapter Four

Sexual tension. Yes, I have it. I caught it unexpectedly, like hepatitis B. I caught it at the Spring Fling. I thought I was going with my old friend, Dylan Madsen, but he turned into a prince in the middle of the evening. I have no experience with princes except on the cover of *People*. The thing is this: Dylan asked me to the Spring Fling probably because Mary Dalgleish had already been asked by Barry Spillman (Mary and Barry—ha!), who had just broken up with Ellie Haslip, who ended up being asked by Ted Lamont, who I had thought would ask me. The domino effect. Joe Garfield asked Sarah—as everyone including Sarah knew he would. We all went together in a hired limousine. No problem there. No problem at dinner. Just the usual gossip, insults, retold movie plots, discussions on which fork was for what, only it was all more polite. Tuxedos and fancy gowns with spaghetti straps have their civilizing effect.

It was at the dance, after we'd had a group picture taken, and after Mary was named Spring Fling Queen, and after Joe laughed too hard while drinking the punch and it came out of his nose. . . . the band started up with some too romantic, slow, slow music, and before I knew it, Dylan and I were on the dance floor slow dancing for the first time ever. He pulled me in close, and I watched glimmering ceiling lights spin the room over his shoulder. He wore cologne. I couldn't stop swallowing. I felt giddy. I pulled back a little and looked up at his face. He looked older, transformed, princelike . . . hot. "This is a little weird," I said. "I mean, you and me—"

He grinned, said, "I like it," and pulled me in again. "I like you and me."

I smiled into his shoulder. Let high school never end.

But in real life, away from the music, when I'm wearing my khakis, this new level of our friendship—a more passionate friendship, or whatever it is—it makes me nervous. What are we, anyway? We only kissed once in my front hall a few weeks ago.

For half an hour.

Sexual tension. Major problemo. I'm spending too much time in front of the mirror wondering if I should wear some makeup, more makeup, or no makeup. I try on dozens of tops, different necklaces. It's only a yearbook signing party and I feel crazy.

"Can't we kiss and be friends too?" I ask the mirror. Even as I speak, I know it's a major philosophical question. Stop, stop, stop. Don't think.

In the bedroom I sweep hairy Maude into my arms and say, "Maudie, I'm in love with Dylan." Our tongues accidentally meet and I throw her on the bed and brush my teeth for another five minutes, trying not to gag.

I can hear Dylan and Sarah laughing in front of his house when I step outside. Clutching my yearbook, I sprint across front lawns, jumping low hedges.

"It's Mira-me-deara." Dylan grins.

Major meltdown. "Hi," I gush. "Sorry I'm late." He used to call me by my last name: Kent or Kent girl. Now it's Mira or Mira-me-deara.

"You're not late." Dylan grins.

"She is too," Sarah says as she opens the back door of Dylan's car.

"Don't you get carsick in the back?" I sit in the back when the three of us go anywhere.

"Not anymore." A goofy smile. "Besides, I'll just vomit and be done with it."

"That'll be good." Dylan climbs in behind the wheel.

I'm still standing out in the driveway. "I can sit in the back," I say.

Dylan leans across the front seat. "Get in," he says, slapping the passenger seat. "Let her hurl."

Sarah giggles.

"This is stupid," I say, but I get in.

She leans forward. "Besides, the two of you look so cute together."

"Sarah!" Dylan and I say it at the same time.

She falls back, laughing.

Dylan turns the key in the ignition and the radio blasts Weezer. Sarah sings along, leaning forward, beating the cadence on our shoulders.

We drive down Virginia Street. Maybe it's the lyrics or Sarah's nasal singing voice, or just the new excitement between us, but Dylan and I burst into snarking laughter and don't stop until the song ends.

When we're headed west on South Temple, Sarah yells over the radio: "Turn it down a minute."

Dylan lowers the volume.

"Time to get to business." Her head is almost in the front seat. "Tell him, Mira." She nudges me.

"Now?"

"Why not?"

"What?" Dylan asks. "Tell me what?"

"Well, I—"

"Mira found out her father's name and—"

"Really?" Dylan glances at me.

"She wants to contact him but all she has is his name. No address. No phone. No e-mail."

"Your mom finally told you?"

"No, I—"

"No, she found a marriage certificate in an old family album. Actually, *I* found it—"

I interrupt: "His name—"

"It isn't even Ambrose. Her mom didn't even give her his real first name. I'm the one who thought of doing a Web search, but the problem is—" Sarah stops when

Dylan brakes suddenly and parks at the side of the street. "Why are we stopping?" she asks.

Dylan turns in his seat. "Will you be quiet for a minute? I keep asking Mira questions and you keep answering."

Sarah raises her eyebrows. "She's answering too slowly. I'm trying to keep a lively pace going here." She sits back.

I snort.

"Besides, I prefer third-person narratives, don't you?" Sarah rattles on.

Dylan smirks at her. "I'd just like to hear the story from Mira."

"Okay, enough about me." Pause. I know what's coming: "What do *you* think of me?" She laughs at herself. "Okay, Mira, tell it—"

"It's all really weird—" I begin.

"That's an understatement," Sarah interrupts.

"Shut up!" Dylan glares at her in the rearview mirror.

I talk with my hands, shaping the albums in midair, touching his arm when I speak my father's name. I tell him about our unproductive Web search. I don't have to ask him anything.

He breaks in. "I can find him. I'll do it tonight."

Sarah moves between us again. "Told you," she says to me.

I swallow. I want to ask if he could get into trouble,

but I bite my lip. I don't really want to know the answer. "Are you sure?" I ask.

He nods. "Absolutely positive."

I cup my hands over my lips. "Ohmygosh, this is really happening."

We've turned into the parking lot across the street from the high school and before we come to a full stop, Joe Garfield taps on the back window. Sarah lowers it and in an efficient adult voice says, "Young man, panhandlers are not allowed in this parking lot, but I have a form here"—she holds up her yearbook—"and if you fill it out, the Salt Lake City school board and the city council could issue a permit—"

Joe clamps his hand over her mouth. "Shut up, Sullivan. You were supposed to pick me up at Hires at seven-fifteen. It is now"—he looks at his watch—"eight-oh-seven."

Sarah's eyes bug out above his hand. "Oops." It comes out muffled. "I forgot."

Joe nods and opens the door and Sarah gets out. "So did you beam yourself here?" she asks.

"You are so full of bullcrap. You know that?" The edge of his mouth turns up. No one can stay mad at Sarah. "Total bullcrap," he says.

"You like it?" She leans toward him and does the blinking thing.

Joe growls at her. Then he turns to us. "You guys coming?"

"Go ahead," Dylan says. "We'll be there in a minute."

We watch their backs as they cross the street toward the high school. Dylan turns in his seat. "The rules have changed," he says.

"You really smell good," I say without thinking.

He grins. "Daisy said I smelled like Easter candy." Daisy is his three-year-old niece.

I nod. "What rule?"

"You sit in the front seat, not Sarah."

"I've become the alpha female? Is there such a thing? Or is there only an alpha male? But when you think about it, between Sarah and me, she is definitely more alpha than I am. I'm kind of alfalfa. I'm hay." I make eye contact. "You really smell good," I say.

He kisses me, his hand on my cheek. I kiss him back.

A group of kids see us from a few cars away and howl their approval.

Dylan grins. "I guess we better go in."

"No, let's not—do you mind? Let's go do the search. I don't want to wait any longer."

On the way home he asks me more questions about my father. I want to show him the albums but realize I've left them at Sarah's house. "I'll show you tomorrow," I say.

He pulls into his garage. "Come on," he says. "It'll just take a few minutes."

I follow him into the house. His mother and grandmother are in the family room watching the news. "Hi," I say.

"Hi, guys." His mom gestures us over. "Come and sit down with us. Nana made Key lime pie."

"It's good," Nana tempts us. An afghan in progress lies in her lap. It is almost the identical pale green of the pie. I like this coincidence.

"Sounds fabulous," I can't help saying.

"Thanks, Mom, but I want to teach Mira how to play backgammon. Do you know if Dad is online?"

So Dylan is going to break a few rules. Otherwise why would he tell this little lie?

His mom shrugs. "Probably, but it's about time he joins the living, so boot him off. Ha, I just made a little computer joke. Get it? *Boot* him off."

"Don't quit your day job, Mom." Dylan heads down the hall.

"Save us some of that pie," I say eagerly. Even I could have put the search off for a piece of Key lime pie. I follow Dylan.

Dylan's dad, Neal, looking disheveled from painting, is at the computer in the study.

"Why don't you teach her with the board set?" he asks. "The board set is just the same."

Dylan looms behind Neal's chair, his hands in his pockets. "I haven't seen you play a board game in seven years." He points at the screen. "Here, move it here."

I lean over the side of the desk and see that his dad really is playing backgammon online. "I thought you were working," I say.

"I am working," his dad says. "I'm a backgammon executive."

"Our turn." Dylan shoves his elbow in his dad's

shoulder. "Besides, Mom says it's time for you to join the humanoids."

"Just let me finish this game!" Neal tussles with Dylan over the screen.

I once read that everyone with a large house has at least one room to glorify himself, and this study glorifies Neal Madsen. The walls are filled with awards from governmental agencies, plaques, commendations, photos of him with local dignitaries. One cabinet is filled with ski trophies from his college days. There's a photo of him and the governor shaking hands. "I wonder if the governor plays backgammon online."

"Don't hassle me, Mira." His face turns up. "Ha! I beat the bum." He stands up. "You clear the screen," he says to Dylan. "Don't use my Yahoo ID. I have a very high playing score and I don't want it ruined." He grasps my shoulder as he comes around the desk. "The governor is a Tetris man," he says in a stage whisper. "He's completely addicted. Very unstable." One side of his lip curves up. "That isn't his real hair either."

"I'll tell everyone I know," I say.

"Good girl." He's out the door. "Where's my pie?" he yells from the hallway.

I pull up a chair next to Dylan. He has already cleared the backgammon game and is into a search engine I don't recognize. "What's this?"

"Don't ask." He bites his bottom lip, concentrating on the screen.

"Is it against the law?" I wasn't going to ask these

questions, but they spill out. "How did you learn to do this?"

He pushes the Enter key with his index finger and sits back. "My dad taught me." His hand comes down on my bare arm. "Watch this—"

The screen is displaying numbers and words at a dizzying pace. Then it stops and there is my father's name, Paul Earl Weissmann; his address in Dallas, Texas; his business address; his telephone numbers at home and at work; and an e-mail address. "Pay dirt," Dylan says.

I touch the screen with my fingers as if to keep the information from disappearing. "Ohmygosh."

"He makes a lot of money." Dylan points at his bank account. "And look at the property he owns. Here, it's listed right here."

I lean forward. "Wow—this is not your ordinary Yahoo search. It's magic!"

Dylan grins. "Not exactly. Do you want to see his medical records? Look, he had kidney stones a few years ago, and he suffered from hemorrhoids—" His smile is twisted.

"Ohmygosh, I don't want to know this much. Just copy off the address and phone number and you know— I don't want to know all his private stuff." I'm rocking in my chair, fists under my chin, elbows hugging my body. "Don't tell me any more!"

"You don't want to see if he has a criminal history? A

few misdemeanors? I can even call up his traffic record!" Dylan's laughing and pushing keys.

"Don't!" I grab his hands. "Stop. Just the e-mail address and the—"

He pushes a key. "Printing!"

"Thank you." I slump sideways on his shoulder. "Thank you, thank you. I owe you."

I spend the rest of the evening at the Madsens', the sheet of paper with my father's vital statistics folded tightly in the pocket of my jeans. We eat the rest of the Key lime pie, play pool in the basement, and watch a movie. We kiss for exactly ten minutes on my front porch. I like to kiss Dylan Madsen. I like the smell of him. I like it that he is my old friend and my new boyfriend.

"Are you going to e-mail him tonight?" Dylan turns back at the edge of the lawn. We have already said good night.

"Not now. I have to think of what to say. Maybe tomorrow."

He nods and lopes toward his house, hands in his pockets. "Keep me in the loop. This is cool, but he *is* a total stranger."

I wish he hadn't warned me like everyone else has.

The front rooms of the house are dark, but I see a blue glow coming from the direction of Mom's study. I stand in the doorway. She and Bella are arm in arm on the sofa, watching some scary movie. "Hi," I say, and they both screech as if they're seeing the devil himself. Bella asks me to sit down, but I tell them I'm going to bed, that I'm tired.

The truth is I *am* tired, but I'm excited too, and I lie awake with Maude snuggled into the small of my back. The paper with Daddy's phone number has grown sweaty in the palm of my hand. The creases are already worn from my opening and closing it so many times. I lie awake through Dr. Sullivan's Explorer alarm going off. I watch the digital numbers of my alarm clock count minute by minute. It's after eleven here. I wonder what time it is in Dallas. I wonder what his voice sounds like. I would like to hear his voice. Is it deep? Lighthearted? Is it growly like Dylan's dad's? Is it like Dylan's? I can't remember your voice, Daddy.

I switch on the bedside lamp and pull the phone onto the bed. Maude looks up briefly and resettles herself on top of my leg. Once again, I unfold the paper. I take a deep breath and begin to dial his number. I just want to hear his voice. I hesitate before pushing the last digit. It rings several times. Maybe he isn't even home. Maybe he's out of town.

He picks up: "Hello."

My mother opens the door and says, "Mira?" Her voice knocks the breath right out of me. I drop the phone into its cradle.

"I didn't mean to startle you." She looks hard at me. "You okay?"

"Of course," I say. I try to laugh it off, but it sounds strangled and artificial.

"Who were you talking to?"

"Dylan. I forgot to tell him something." I stink at lying.

She smiles. "You were just with him."

I nod.

"Well, I just wanted to say good night."

"Good night."

She blows me a kiss and shuts the door.

I stare at the phone and jump when it rings. I already know who it is. I think I know. I pick it up.

"Hello."

"Mira?" It's that voice again—his voice. "Mira? Are you there? Mirabelle?

"Talk to me. Mira?"

I can't talk. I can hardly breathe. I hang up the phone. Will it ring again? Daddy knows my number—or did he star 69 me? Maybe he heard Mom call my name. My heart still races and I keep swallowing down a rising anxiety. Was calling him a mistake? I turn off the light and pull the blanket over my head. I like the way my father called my name: "Mira, Mirabelle, Mira."

Tomorrow I will e-mail him and try to explain myself.

Maude licks my face when I lie back on the pillow. I push her away.

I fall into a whirling dream where I am dancing with Daddy, who wears his wedding suit and smiles at me, but then he becomes Dylan with his own smile. I lean forward to kiss him, my eyes shut, and when they open I have kissed Daddy, not Dylan. I have kissed him like a lover. I cannot keep them straight. I love them both, but not the same way. Surely not the same way. I have to keep my eyes open in this dream, which is fraught with romantic danger. I have to keep my eyes open.

Chapter Five

Early, Early Sunday Morning

To: pw@wbrokerage.net
From: mira618@hotmail.com

Dear Paul Weissmann,
I called you last night. I wanted to hear your voice. I'm sorry I
hung up when you called back, but my mother walked in and
I didn't want her to know who was at the other end of the line.
She would have freaked. She has been reluctant to tell me
very much about you—I think to ensure your privacy—but now
that I'm getting older, I would really like to know more. I found
your name in an old family album and my friend, Dylan, was
able to find your e-mail through a Net search. I know you live
in Dallas. You probably have a family. If you don't want to
write, I'll understand. I liked hearing your voice. I'm glad you
called me back. Did you * 69 me? Anyway, if you feel you can,
I hope you will write me back.

Sincerely,
Mira

P.S. My hair is the same color as yours—RED.
P.P.S. You have a nice voice.

To: mira618@hotmail.com
From: pw@wbrokerage.net

My dear Mirabelle,
Receiving your e-mail this morning is the best thing that has
happened to me since the day of your birth. The agreement your
mother and I made was unwise. I regret it and have regretted it for
several years, because you, Mirabelle dear, you are my only family.
Since your mother left, I have buried myself in work. I tried to find
you a few years ago without success, so you can imagine my joy
in hearing from you. I did not * 69 you. It was caller ID. I had to
smile that you didn't think about it. I imagine your mother would
not go in for such a technological advancement. I see by your area
code that you live in Utah in the region around Salt Lake City. I
have had layovers in Salt Lake City. It's a beautiful place; I can see
why your mother chose to live there. I once stopped long enough
to tour Brigham Young's house and the attached house with all the
gables, one for each wife. Salt Lake City is the crossroads of the
West, isn't it? Someday, you and I will meet at that crossroads.
I will not call again; it is too awkward for you. But I would be
happy to have a correspondence with you. There is so much
to catch up on. I want to hear about your life. I hope you are
happy. I'll wait to hear from you.

Love,
Daddy

P. S. That red hair comes from your grandmother Abigail
McDonald Weissmann.

To: pw@wbrokerage.net
From: mira618@hotmail.com

Dear Daddy,
I can't believe you've traveled through Salt Lake City. Please,
please let me know when you have a layover at the airport.

I live only twenty minutes from there and could meet you in person even if it is only for a few minutes. It would be a dream come true. You are right about Mom's dislike of modern technology. She won't even let me have a cell phone. Bella, on the other hand, has all the latest gadgets because of her real estate business. I feel lucky to have a computer and access to the Internet. I'm so grateful to have found you, dear Daddy. I have wanted to know about you forever.

All my love,
Your Mirabelle

To: mira618@hotmail.com
From: pw@wbrokerage.net

My dear Mirabelle,
I am reluctant to tell you this, because it might be better to wait, but I do have a one-hour layover in Salt Lake City this Wednesday evening at 7:00 on my way to Minneapolis. My cautious nature tells me this is too soon to meet; although I have to say I may be even more excited to see you again than you are to see me. Still, it may be wise to get better acquainted through e-mail and wait to meet at a later date. I know I have a meeting just before Thanksgiving in Minneapolis again, and it might be more appropriate to meet at that time. In any case, we will meet one of these days. My dear Mirabelle, you have made me happier than you can know.

Love,
Daddy

To: pw@wbrokerage.net
From: mira618@hotmail.com

Daddy, we have to meet this very Wednesday. How could I put it off until Thanksgiving? How could you? Please, Daddy.

Love,
Your Mirabelle

To: mira618@hotmail.com
From: pw@wbrokerage.net

Mirabelle, if you're sure. I think you should bring a friend (certainly your mother would want you to do this). I don't want to impose myself on you. If you should change your mind for any reason, then don't come. I will understand. Just knowing you through e-mail is more than I ever expected to have.

All my love,
Daddy

To: pw@wbrokerage.net
From: mira618@hotmail.com

Daddy, I'll be there Wednesday evening at 7:00 in the baggage area. I'll be the one with the goofy smile on my face. I'll be humming and twirling, because I'm meeting you. See you then!

Your little girl,
Mira

Chapter Six

Sunday

At four o'clock this morning I couldn't wait any longer, and I e-mailed Daddy. I got an e-mail right back, and so we wrote back and forth. Then I was so excited that I was going to meet him in less than a week that I listened to the radio for a while and finally drifted off.

I am startled into wakefulness by the ringing telephone. I pick it up.

"Well? Did he get it for you?" It's Sarah, beginning in mid-conversation.

"What?"

"Did I wake you?" She doesn't wait for an answer. "Geez, it's eight o'clock."

"It's Sunday!"

"I know, and church starts at nine o'clock." She stops. "For those of us who actually *go to church.*"

"Oh, don't get self-righteous on me."

"Did Dylan get your dad's e-mail for you?"

The whole night comes back to me and I am fully awake. "Yes! Yes, he did."

"I told you he'd do it."

"Yes, and I have so much to tell you. We've been e-mailing since four o'clock this morning. Well, not the *whole* time, but—"

"Ohmygosh!"

"Sarah, he's so nice. He lives in Dallas and he—"

Sarah's voice on the phone becomes muffled but I can hear her yell, "I'm coming!" Then she's back on with me. "I have to go to breakfast. We've got to meet. We're having the grandparents for lunch so I won't be ready to see you until four or so."

"Come to my house," I say. "Tell Dylan to come too."

"Okay, see you then."

We hang up and I swoop a surprised Maude up in bed and spin her around. "You know who loves you? Do you? Me, that's who." She barks, and I get up to let her outside.

Mom and Bella are taken with spring fever and suggest we have brunch at the Homestead in Midway, about forty minutes' drive away. "Let's wear skirts," Mom says.

"Floral," Bella says.

"Geez," I say. They're always coming up with fashion ideas I hate. Then we vote and, of course, I always lose. "What about hats? Don't you want to go all the way and wear hats as well?"

"Too much of a good thing," Bella says, smirking.

Mom stands by the window. "It's almost eighty degrees right now." She swivels around. "Do we *own* any hats?"

"I'll bet Bella has hats hidden somewhere." I pick at the grapes in a bowl on the table.

"I do," Bella says, "but I don't think this is a hat decade." She fills Maude's bowl with canned dog food. "In fact, we haven't really had a hat decade since the fifties."

"Yeah, and that's the last time they had a skirt decade too," I say.

They both look at me and chirp: "We're wearing skirts."

"Okay, okay. I get it. I don't like it, but I get it." I head toward the stairs. "I live in a female dictatorship: a despot, a prime minister, and a peasant."

"I'm the despot," Bella say.

"Prime minister—*moi*!" Mom says.

I turn in the doorway and droop my shoulders. "I know my place," I say, "and I accept it."

They jeer. "Off with her head!" Bella cries.

I run up the stairs, giggling. Nothing could make me unhappy today.

Bella drives the Mercedes up Parley's Canyon. The three of us look like spring personified, but I have to admit we look pretty good too. The mountains are especially green because of the heavy snows we had this winter, the sky is intensely cobalt, and yellow wildflowers bloom abundantly along the side of the road.

Mom says aloud what I'm thinking. "It's beautiful."

Bella hums.

In the backseat, I lean my head against the window and see my red hair in the reflection. Red hair like my grandmother Abigail's.

"Do I have other grandparents?" I ask aloud.

"You have a grandmother, yes. Abigail. She had the reddest hair. I only met her once, at the wedding," Mom says. "Well, twice, actually."

I'm surprised that Mom gives me Abigail's real name. "Is she alive?"

"I don't know that." There's sadness in Mom's voice. "She was about ten years older than Bella. I imagine she is."

"Maybe someday I'll meet her," I say.

Mom looks out the window. Bella concentrates on driving. My legacy is silence. I will ask Daddy about Abigail.

At the restaurant, we sit at a window that overlooks the trout pond and the garden behind it. I notice the men at other tables looking at my mother. She's so pretty. "Do you think you'll ever marry again?" I ask.

Her spoon of asparagus soup is poised midway to her mouth. She lowers it, blushing. She knows that men look at her. "I don't think so," she says.

"You were twenty when you got married?"

"Too young," Bella says.

"Twenty," Mom says. "Too young for sure."

"I'll be twenty in four years."

That makes Mom choke on her soup.

Bella says to her, "Put a stake through her heart now."

Mom is coughing and smiling at the same time.

Bella raises her fork. "You want me to do it?"

"I'm not getting married at twenty," I say. "Twenty-two, when Dylan gets back from his mission."

That makes their jaws drop. "Have you talked about this?" Mom asks.

"Not yet." I smile.

"You'll have to become a Mormon," Bella says. "He won't marry you if you're not Mormon. That means you'll have to go to church every Sunday for three hours, not the once in a while you do now. Are you ready for a lifetime of three-hour Sunday meetings? Lord!"

"It's not one meeting; they're three different meetings, one right after another."

"It's three hours!"

I give her my look.

"Well, it is!" Bella gives me *her* look.

Someone begins playing the piano in an adjoining dining room. They play the music from *Sense and Sensibility*.

"I like this," Mom says.

"Dylan is a lovely boy," Bella says. "If I were forty years younger—"

"Pleeeze." I roll my eyes.

During her lobster pesto, Mom says, "We did correspond—Abby and I. I sent her snapshots of you."

I have a mouthful of garlic mashed potatoes and can

only nod at her. She's volunteering information. Safe information.

"Then after the divorce, I took you to see her. You were three and she was crazy about you, wasn't she?" She looks over at Bella for support. Bella nods.

"Where did she live?"

"Arkansas," Mom says, and at the same time, Bella says, "Alabama." They look at each other.

"It was one of those *A* states," Bella says.

"It was Arkansas—Bill Clinton was once governor—"

"Maybe it was Alaska." I'm enjoying this. "Alaska begins with *A*. So does Arizona."

"It was Arkansas." Mom's lips press together. "She lives in Arkansas."

The two of them look a little foolish. "Must have been an *A*-loving family. She's *Abigail* and she names her son *Ambrose* and they live in *Arkansas*. Dr. Seuss could have done something with that!"

Bella wipes her mouth with her napkin. "They were a class-A family. What can we say? Do you want that chocolate cake for dessert?"

It's a diversion all three of us want. "Yes. Chocolate cake is good."

After brunch we drive up through Daniel's Canyon and try to get lost, a favorite game of mine, but it's impossible. Eventually we hit a sign that points to Heber or Midway or Park City. We stop at the outlet mall in Park City and look for shoes. We all try some on but no one buys. Finally Bella says we better head home before Maude bursts her bladder.

Back at home I have just enough time to change my clothes before I hear Mom let Dylan and Sarah in. "Come on upstairs," I yell down to them.

When they're in my room and the door is shut I whisper loudly, "I wrote my dad and he wrote me back."

"Hey, nice to see you too," Dylan says, leaning over to kiss my cheek.

"I want to read the e-mails," Sarah says.

"He is so nice. Really so nice." I boot up my laptop at the desk and go to my mail. They read over my shoulder.

"You called him? Tell me you didn't call him." Dylan's incredulous.

"She called him," Sarah says.

"I just wanted to hear his voice," I squeak. "I forgot about caller ID. We don't have it—Mom and I don't have it—"

"I can't believe you called him. Don't you read the news? You called a guy you know nothing about?" Dylan's holding his forehead.

"I didn't talk to him. I hung up. Besides, he's my dad."

"But he's still a stranger! There might be a good reason your mom doesn't want you around him." Dylan leans on the desk, his face close to mine, and it's infuriating.

"He does sound nice," Sarah says, continuing to read.

"Anybody can be nice in an e-mail," Dylan says. He reads along with Sarah. I wish I hadn't invited them up. I wish I hadn't invited Dylan, anyway.

"Ohmygosh," Sarah says.

"You can't meet him," Dylan says. "He already knows you live in Salt Lake. Crap, Mira, what were you thinking?"

I shoot up out of my chair. "I want to meet my father and I wish you'd stop sounding like some old-fart parent. I'm the one who suggested the meeting. He didn't. Get off my back."

"He did suggest that she bring friends," Sarah says. "That's a good sign. I mean, he's being cautious."

"Oh, right." Dylan is skeptical.

"I'll go," Sarah says.

"Thank you," I say.

"I'm going; what good would you do?" Dylan asks Sarah.

"My mother dated Charles Manson and lived to tell the tale." Sarah sticks her chin out.

"My father is not Charles Manson or anyone like him." I shove her shoulder.

"She did?" Dylan turns into Gullible Guy.

"Dylan! Charles Manson must be Bella's age!" I say.

Sarah lets out a whoop. "Gotcha!"

Dylan looks rueful. "Well, the guy had magnetism. Charisma."

Sarah snorts.

"You guys—"

"We'll both go with you," Sarah says. "Your dad invited your friends along and we're your friends. One of us is your *boyfriend*."

"Yeah." Dylan smiles out of the side of his mouth and throws his arm around my neck. "Guess which one."

I squeeze him.

"I'm outta here," Sarah says.

I'm pulling Bella's homemade lemon ice cream out of the freezer when Bella walks in, all businesslike. She nods briefly at Dylan and Sarah. "Is Maude upstairs in your room?" she asks.

"No, we locked her in the downstairs bathroom, don't you remember?" I set the cold canister in the sink.

"That's what I thought, but she isn't in there and the door was open. I thought you might have taken her upstairs with you." Her face has a worried, pinched look. "We've been home half an hour and we can't find her anywhere. Your mom's taken her car out to look along Virginia Street." She pulls the lapel of her jacket across her neck as if to protect herself from some awful reality. "She doesn't usually disappear like this."

"She wouldn't be out on Virginia Street," I say. Maude's the kind of dog who likes human attention. She's usually right at your heels.

"We'll go have a look," Dylan volunteers. He rises out of his chair.

Sarah stands up too. "We could make signs and post them, so people know she's missing."

Bella sees the canister. "Have your ice cream first."

Who is she kidding? We tell her we'll have some after the search.

Sarah organizes us. "I'll go east all the way to the

university. Dylan, you go west to the avenues—"
Yammer yammer. "We'll meet back here at five-thirty.
Let's synchronize watches." She holds up her wrist.

Dylan's lips curve into a sneer. "Let's just meet here in
an hour, if that's all right with you, Double-Oh-Seven."

"Right!" Sarah salutes him and heads to the front
door.

Dylan touches my arm. "Later," he says.

Bella sits on the porch in case the dog returns on her
own. I run up to my bedroom just to make sure Maude
isn't sleeping in my bedcovers, a favorite nap spot for her,
but she isn't there or in any of her other hangouts. From
Mom's study, I walk out through the French doors to the
backyard, which is ablaze with peonies: pink, rose, and
white. Some of the blossoms are so heavy that they droop
to the ground. Maude chose a glorious day to be out and
about. I call her name, expecting her to scramble out from
some hiding place, but everything is still. I walk back
through the house. "I'm heading north," I tell Bella, who
still sits on the step. "Maybe she's up in Arlington Hills."

Bella nods, but I can tell she's not feeling hopeful.
"She's never been gone this long," she says. "I'm afraid
someone's stolen her."

"People steal dogs?" I've never heard of such a thing.

She covers her eyes with her hand to look up at me.
"Good dogs—they do."

I think about this as I walk toward Alta Street, and for
the first time, I worry I may not see Maude again. I call

her name more fiercely. Maude has slept in my bedroom since I was eight. Who would steal a pet?

I've walked three blocks north, when Mom, in her Honda, finds me by the church. "I'm going to Arlington Hills," I say.

"I've been there," she calls from the car. "Get in. We'll go around University Park."

I hesitate. "She'd have to cross South Temple to get there." It's a busy street.

Mom nods. I get in. She lets me out at the park, and I jog around its circumference, checking the tennis courts. Mom drives up and down Fraternity Row, asking pedestrians if they've seen a fluffy white dog. We drive down South Temple and across Thirteenth East to Fourth South and come back along University. No Maude.

We're out longer than an hour. When we return, Dylan and Sarah are making signs at the kitchen table to hang at street corners. When I stand next to Dylan's chair, he puts his arms around my waist. Sarah gives us a hard look.

"Offer a reward," Bella says. She is spooning lemon ice cream into bowls. "Offer five hundred dollars."

Sarah's mouth drops open. "I wouldn't offer that much for my little brother," she says.

"Neither would I." Dylan and I say this at the same time and grin at each other.

"Tut tut," Mom says, but she smiles.

Even Bella's face relaxes a little. "It's too beautiful to

eat inside. I'm taking these out to the patio." She lifts the tray with the bowls of ice cream and heads through the French doors. "Come now," she calls. "It melts quickly in this sun."

"Do you know that triangular relationships are problematic?" Sarah asks as we move outside. "Like *three* friends, for instance. One is always on the outside. It shifts, but one is always on the outside. Like upstairs in your room, Dylan and I were on the same side, but now—"

"What's your point?" Dylan and I are in simultaneous mode. It's the second time, and we snort.

Sarah says, "Yuk yuk," and sneers.

Mom leans over to Sarah, her whisper conspiratorial: "This too shall pass."

"Not soon enough." Sarah rolls her eyes.

Bella's ice cream melts in our mouths and melts our tension. For a few minutes we can forget about Maude and triangular relationships. I blow a kiss to Sarah, who sits across from me.

"Kiss-up!" she says.

Bella laughs. "You two—" She shakes her head.

Dylan is trying to convince Mom that *The Scarlet Letter* shouldn't be taught in high school. "It's pointless," he says. "What do teenagers know about adultery and the wages of sin? Take Hester's child, Pearl—what the heck is she all about?" He stops. His forehead contracts into a squint. "Whoa." It comes out low, under his breath almost. We follow his gaze to the peony bed.

"What?" Mom asks.

He stands slowly, pushing his chair back, and takes a few steps away from the table, his face drained of color. "It's Maude."

The rest of us see her at once. Mom muffles a cry with her hand. Sarah lets out a pinched little scream. Bella gasps.

Maude is buried up to her head, blended among the white peonies, her eyes glazed in a dead stare.

"Take her out, take her out!" My hands flap up and down.

Dylan walks over to the peony bed and stoops down, digging out the dog with his hands. Mom helps him. The rest of us stand watching.

"Is she dead?" I ask, knowing the answer.

Dylan speaks: "Yes."

Mom nods.

The dirt is loose, and it isn't long before they uncover Maude's front paws, which are tied together with barbed wire.

Who could be so cruel? I've crossed my arms and hidden my hands in my armpits. It is sunny and warm, but I feel as if I need protection from the cold.

Sarah speaks my thoughts: "What maniac would do this?"

"I'm calling the police," Bella says, taking her cell phone out of her pocket.

When they have finished digging, Dylan lifts Maude's

body onto the lawn. Her back feet are also tied with wire. Mom begins to untwist the wire, but Dylan stops her. "Better let the police see her as she is," he says.

Sarah and I sit on the lawn with them. Maude's usually immaculate white fur is packed with dirt. Her neck twists at an odd angle from her body. "It looks as if her neck is broken," I say. My eyes burn behind my lids, but I don't cry.

Two uniformed police officers come and look at the dog. One is Officer Cody, who has a crew cut and a little scar that splits one eyebrow. Officer Hernandez, the one with a mustache, has big perspiration stains under his arms. They ask the obvious questions: Do you have neighbors who might be angry with you or the dog? How long was the dog missing? Have you seen strangers in the neighborhood? Are there any kids in the neighborhood who might do this? Did the dog bite people? Do you have wire like this in your house or garage? Was the dog out?

Bella tells them the dog was locked in the bathroom.

"Was the house locked?" Officer Hernandez wants to know.

"Yes," we all three say, although I'm not sure the doors from Mom's study to the patio were locked. Hernandez sees me glance at Mom. He raises his eyebrows at me. "You think something different?" he asks me.

"Sometimes I forget to lock it, but I don't think I was the last one who let Maude out this morning."

"Well, young lady, if you don't keep the doors locked—"

Bella's neck stiffens. "Young *man,* she doesn't need a lecture about the obvious; besides, I let Maude out just before we left and the door was locked." She emphasizes "locked" and gives him one of her disdainful glares.

The police hang around another hour—it seems longer. They examine Maude and take notes. I notice that Officer Hernandez never looks directly at Bella when he needs to ask her a question. Bella's disgusted with both of them, because they are so useless and because they leave the red light on their squad car blinking "like an advertisement for a whorehouse." These are her words. She spits out complaints in undertones that are not meant for the officers' ears.

Officer Cody takes some pictures.

Mom fills out forms.

The squad car parked in front of the house raises curiosity on the block and soon Dr. Sullivan is looking Maude over, but even he can't save a dog that's been dead a couple of hours. He stands with one arm around Sarah, who cries silently.

I wish my dad were here.

When the officers are gone, Dylan and Dr. Sullivan remove the wires from Maude's paws and bury her next to the rose garden. Mom asks if they will pull out the white peony bush; she'll replace it with another color. They throw the bush into the garbage.

Soon everyone is gone. Bella, Mom, and I each disappear into our own corner of the house for a while. I lie on my bed with the coverlet over me, not bothering to take my shoes off. Maude's smell is on my pillow. Her favorite squeaky toy, an orange rubber lion with a red crown on its head, lies across the room under the window. I fall asleep crying.

My dreams are without plot, filled with familiar images of people I know. Maude, Dylan, and Sarah play basketball in an open field with a ball that has an incredible bounce. I run to get the ball when it goes out of play. Bella drives a Batmobile with Mom dressed as Robin. Then there is a stairway in the same field where Dylan and Sarah played basketball and it leads up, way up, and at the top stands my dad in his wedding suit and he's holding Maude, who's yapping wildly. "I will never let Maude be taken away from me," he says.

I wake up, heart pounding, perspiring, suffocating in my clothes. My bedroom is dark and disorienting. I turn on the light and pick up my laptop from the floor. I send my dad an e-mail telling him about the horrible day.

Within a half hour, I receive an e-mail back:

To: mira618@hotmail.com
From: pw@wbrokerage.net

My dear Mirabelle,
I'm so sorry to hear about your poor little Maude's death. It is hard to imagine such an unconscionable act on an innocent animal. It's alarming too that someone broke into the house to get the dog. It's as if someone has been watching your house

and knows when the three of you leave. I urge you to be most careful. I don't want anything to happen to my little girl and her loved ones. Wish I could be there to comfort you in person.

All my love,
Daddy

It's sweet that he wants to be with me. I hadn't thought, though, of someone watching our house, and it spooks me. Why would someone be watching our house? And then a terrible thought comes to me. Maybe Daddy is watching our house. I want to deny the thought, but I remember Dylan's shock that I had let my dad know that I live in Salt Lake City. It's only a little after ten, so I call Dylan's cell.

When he answers I say, "I think I'd like to know if my dad has a criminal record now."

"O-*kay*," he says slowly. "What made you change your mind?"

"You keep saying I should be more careful—"

"He doesn't have a criminal record. I looked it up after Maude was killed."

"I told you!" I say.

He laughs. "You weren't that sure yourself."

"I know," I say, "but he couldn't get to Salt Lake that fast anyway. I only e-mailed him early this morning and he lives in Dallas, right?"

"*Right,* he lives in Dallas; *wrong,* he could have flown in this morning."

"What?"

"I also looked to see what flights arrived from Dallas this morning."

It takes a moment to process what he's saying.

"Mira, are you still there?"

"I'm here," I say. "You looked up flights?"

"Yeah, and there are four that came in before twelve-thirty-five P.M. If he left at six, he could have been here before ten. Although if he came on a nonstop flight, he could have left at nine-forty this morning and arrived before noon."

"Oh" is all I say.

He catches the disappointment in my voice, because he says, "Just because he could have gotten here doesn't mean he did. The guy hasn't had so much as a parking ticket. It's hard to believe he'd go through all that trouble to kill a dog. I really don't think he did it."

"I can't believe you looked all this stuff up," I say.

"I wasn't going to tell you, but you asked."

"Thanks," I say.

After we hang up, I feel gloomy. Maude is dead. I don't entirely trust my dad. This isn't the way I want things to be. I cry into my pillow, wash my face, cry some more, and wash it again.

Later, I go down to find Mom and Bella. They are in Mom's study watching television and cutting into fresh brownies.

"I was just going to come and see if you were awake."

Mom stops when she sees my face, which probably still looks swollen from crying. "Oh, honey." She clasps me in her arms and I begin crying all over again, although I don't mean to. "Oh, sweetie." She strokes and kisses my face and I remember how much I still need my mother.

Chapter Seven

Monday

I'm glad to be up Monday morning. Thoughts of Maude and Daddy and the conflicting emotions they evoke make real sleep impossible. I doze and remember and doze again. The ringing alarm is a relief.

I hear Mom's and Bella's low voices from the stairs but they stop talking when I enter the kitchen, their faces grim.

"What?" I ask, pouring Cheerios into a bowl.

Mom gazes out the window and Bella looks down at the cantaloupe on her plate.

"You guys didn't sleep any more than I did, I'll bet." I sit at the table.

They share one of their excluding glances.

"What?"

"We never went to bed," Mom says.

"We talked." Bella sighs. She looks her age for once.

I notice then that they're wearing the same clothes as the night before. Neither one is dressed for work.

Mom reads what must be a puzzled look on my face. "I called in sick," she says.

"In the last week of school?" This is so unlike her.

"We've been thinking . . ." Bella hesitates and glances at Mom, who nods approval.

I stir sliced bananas into my Cheerios. Sometimes the two of them are so weird.

"How would you like to go to Europe for the summer?" Bella raises her eyebrows to show enthusiasm. Mom tries for a smile, but their anxiety fills the room.

"Alone?"

"No, all of us. You could invite Sarah to come along," Mom says.

Bella picks it up. "Barcelona, Paris, Rome—"

"Or," Mom says, "we could summer on Lake Lugano in southern Switzerland. Just sort of bake ourselves in the sun—"

"Shop till we drop—" Bella again.

Their eagerness for me to like their plan is alarming.

"We could leave as early as next week." Mom sounds unusually perky.

"Next week?" My voice is high, like a distressed bird's. "Right after school is out? I can't go next week!" I think of losing contact with Daddy. And Dylan. Not seeing Dylan for a whole summer. Not hearing from Daddy. "No!" I shout it, and both Mom's and Bella's heads fall back. "I can't just leave." I'm hollering, but I can't help it. "For that matter, I can't believe you're thinking of leaving." I face Mom. "I thought you were signed up for a medieval literature class at the university." Then to Bella: "And you can hardly leave your business for a day without a major panic attack!"

"That's absurd," Bella says. "Judy can carry it for the summer."

"Judy is your secretary! She can't even spell!" I'm spitting *s*s.

"Well then—" Mom's hands flutter in front of her. "Maybe July. You think about it for a while."

"No!" My fist thwacks the table. Dishes clatter.

Mom winces and turns to gaze at the peony patch.

Bella stands, her lips pressed in a tight line, and begins clearing the dishes.

I'm overreacting as usual, but the two of them rushed me with it. They did. They rushed me. I make my voice as soft as I can. "I'll ask Sarah." It's the only form of apology I'm willing to make.

"You told them no? Are you out of your mind?" Sarah is having a hissy fit in the back of Dylan's car. We are on our way to school.

"I don't want to be away all summer." It sounds feeble now.

"Even if it's in *Europe*?" Dylan says.

"Would you go if your parents just sprang it on you?"
I ask.

"In a heartbeat," he says. No romantic side glances or
pauses. He turns right onto South Temple. He's a sorry
excuse for a boyfriend.

"And they invited me along and you still said no?"
Sarah is incredulous. "I don't know if our friendship can
survive this bitter blow."

"I told them I'd think about it," I say.

"Why don't you want to go?" Dylan's voice is curious,
not blaming.

Because I don't want to spend the summer without
you and your heavenly kisses. Instead I say, "I won't be
able to stay in touch with my dad."

Both of them say it at the same time: "Yes you will!"

"E-mail kiosks," Dylan says. "My dad uses them all
the time when he's in Geneva."

Sarah leans forward. "My parents used them when they
went to London. You just pay for how many minutes you
need." She grabs my shoulder. "It's cheap and you can
resume Operation Daddy when you get back."

No one sees my point of view. "But why do they want
to go so suddenly?" I ask. "Usually it takes forever to
plan a trip at our house, and then this morning I get up
and they say, 'Let's go to Europe for the summer.' Don't
you think that's out of character?"

"Stop overanalyzing," Sarah says. "They've had a
trauma and they're freaked out and want to get away. Let

them be whimsical for once in their lives. You benefit and, more importantly, I benefit." She bangs on the ceiling of the car. "I'm going to Europe, me, *moi*. What a day. What a razzle-dazzle day!"

Dylan gives me a sidelong grin. "Are you going to e-mail me too?" he asks.

Okay, I like this better. "Mm-hmm," I murmur.

At school I call Mom from the office. "Sarah and Dylan think I'm crazy for not wanting to go to Europe," I say. "Sarah's been hyperventilating since I told her." I'm using Mrs. Kugel's phone. She's one of the school secretaries.

"So it's okay?" Mom asks.

"Yeah, I guess." I sigh. "But couldn't we wait a couple of weeks?"

"I think so," she says. "We need to get you and Sarah passports." Short pause. "I'm glad, Mira. Thank you."

I don't know why she's so grateful but it makes me feel even guiltier. First I go behind her back about Daddy, and now I've blown up at her over a great offer. "Sorry I was so offended and offensive," I say.

She likes it when I play with words. "No offense taken," she says. "We should have told you—" Pause. "Someone tried to break into our house after you went to bed last night."

"What? When?" For the second time in one morning she takes me by surprise.

"Eileen Dayton called last night after midnight and

said she and the judge could see a figure in our yard from their upstairs bedroom. He was lurking by the French doors in the back. It gives me the willies to think about it." There's a shudder in her voice.

"Did you see him?" How could I have slept through this drama?

"No. Judge Dayton walked through their yard with a baseball bat yelling at the guy at the same time that Bella turned on the backyard lights. Whoever it was ran off."

The Daytons' backyard and ours share a fence with a gate in it. I smile to think of Judge Dayton saving us. He's smaller than I am and in his seventies, although he does have a commanding voice.

"Did Bella see him?"

"She saw a dark figure run to the side of the house, but one of the door handles had been completely broken off." She sighs. "First Maude, then this. I feel like we're being stalked."

It's as if someone has been watching your house. That's what Daddy wrote.

"You think someone wants to hurt us?"

Her voice changes too quickly, becoming too breezy. "Oh, heavens no! I think he's your basic common thief. Bella has all those antiques. It doesn't take a genius to see they're worth something. He could be the same person who killed Maude and thought he'd come back and get the good stuff."

"Well, that isn't *stalked*—a thief doesn't *stalk*," I say. "I mean, *stalking* is something they do in those terrible made-for-women's-TV movies."

She sniggers. "That bad?"

"You better call the police."

"We did, Mira."

"And I thought I didn't sleep."

"You slept and missed the whole thing, and I think that's a good thing."

"What are the police going to do?" Mrs. Snoopdog Kugel looks up from her computer when I ask this question.

Mom sighs. "There's not a lot they can do until a crime is actually committed. They're doing occasional drive-bys. I called the locksmith and he's going to replace the knob and put another lock on my study door, and a man is coming by to check out our security system. It didn't go off."

"That's because we never set it."

"Bella did last night." Her voice changes suddenly. "Shouldn't you be in class?" It's as if she's only just realized I'm at school.

"They're just signing yearbooks. Mrs. Hauptmann brought cinnamon rolls."

"Really?" This goes against her theory that only bad teachers bring treats. She likes Mrs. Hauptmann. "What's she making up for?"

"Oh, Mom." I snicker.

"See you tonight."

"See you."

I hang up. "Somebody tried to break into our house last night," I say to Mrs. Kugel.

She looks away from the computer screen, her face falling into an empathetic droop. "Would you like to talk to a counselor?" This is what she always asks, whether you're short lunch money or your house burns down.

I shake my head.

Sarah and I don't want to eat in the cafeteria and decide to look for Dylan and get him to take us for a hamburger. We head outside to wait for him near his car. He and Joe almost always have their lunch away from campus. We hear a "Whooeee" and turn to see Joe and Dylan running from the north side of the building.

"Just in time, taxi man!" Sarah shouts.

"Girls dig my car," Dylan says to Joe as they approach us.

"Nothing like an old Prizm to get your heart racing," Joe says. He sits in the backseat with Sarah, and I sit in front with Dylan. We are couples, and I am surprised at the surge of happiness this releases.

"Where to, Euro-babe?" Dylan's hand is on my knee.

"Go to Hires so I can eat free," Joe says. "It's the only perk I get for working there."

"What a gentleman." Sarah punches him.

"If it's free, it's good." Joe leans forward suddenly. "Hey, I heard about your dad. That's so cool. Are you going to see him?"

"Wednesday night," I say. We're heading down the hill on Eighth South. Heat shimmers above the road ahead of us. Summer is nearly here. "Don't tell anyone, though. I mean it, Joe."

"Would I tell? I'm Mr. Discreet." He turns to Sarah. "What does *discreet* mean?"

"Joe, really!" I say.

"Just kidding. Are you carrying a flower in a book when you meet him? You know, like in some romantic novel—"

Sarah leans forward. "Sweet Valley High." She and I break up laughing. "I *loved* those books!"

Dylan deadpans: "I know, it was totally my favorite."

"It's not an 'it.' It's dozens of books. A new boyfriend every week."

Joe's voice rises to falsetto. "I love those Sweet Valley High girls. Love 'em, love 'em." He smacks his lips and Sarah elbows him hard.

"Anyway, we don't have to wear flowers or anything else; we both have the same red hair."

Dylan smiles when Joes clucks his tongue. "Oh yes, the red hair. Well, that's it then." Joe sits back. "No flower can compete with that red hair."

"Yeah, I guess," I say. "I'm pretty sure he's safe. I mean, he doesn't sound like a killer."

"How do you know what a killer sounds like?" Dylan swivels his head to back out of the parking space.

I look into my lap. "You know what I mean. Anyway, his e-mails sound so nice. He couldn't possibly be—you know—"

"Freddy freaking Krueger—" Joe says from the back-seat.

Dylan shrugs. "No, but he might be the cool, well-spoken Ted Bundy." He smiles from the corner of his mouth.

He's kidding. But this is my daddy and it's a huge deal. They don't get it; they've always known their fathers.

"I don't think so," I say.

Dylan gives me a sideways glance. "I don't really think so either."

"Somebody tried to break into our house last night," I say, hoping the thief will draw attention away from Daddy and onto a real criminal.

It works. "Last night? I can't believe it," Dylan says.

"Did you call the police again?" Sarah asks.

"Mom and Bella did. Evidently I slept through the whole thing. Bella didn't want to take a chance after the deal with Maude." I don't trust myself to say what the deal with Maude was.

They want to know details. I tell them about the bro-ken lock and then we move on to other break-in stories, real and imagined. When we get to Hires, the carhop comes to the window and Joe orders two doughnuts and a glass of buttermilk.

"Ugh, no way," Sarah says.

"Yeah, I just had buttermilk for the first time last week and I love the stuff."

"Aren't you eating anything besides fat?"

"C'mon, guys, I'm a growing boy. This is the only time in my life when I can eat doughnuts without gaining weight. Do you realize what a gift that is?"

The rest of us order hamburgers and fries with special fry sauce.

"It's not like you guys are health nuts," Joe says.

When the food comes, Sarah tells Joe about going to Europe and he says he has to get in on that.

Dylan starts with his fries. "It seems like a huge—"

I wipe a stray piece from his bottom lip and grin at him. "A huge?"

He swallows a couple of times. "Is it possible that the person who killed Maude could also be trying to get into your house?" He takes a bite out of his hamburger. "Because it seems like a huge coincidence that those two events happened on the same day."

I watch his lips as he speaks. I want to kiss the crumbs off those lips. "I doubt it," I say. I want him to stop talking about this and flirt with me.

Joe is saying something about his desperate desire to see LEGOLAND.

Dylan wipes his mouth with a napkin. "I'll bet your mother and Bella have thought about it." He passes me the fry sauce. His face looks serious. "I think that's why they want to haul you and themselves off to Europe for the summer."

He has my full attention. "You think we're in some kind of danger?"

"I don't know. I think they're worried." He crumples the paper that held his hamburger and sets it out on the tray. "What if I come over and sleep in your mother's study for a couple of nights? My folks would let me. It might make them feel better."

"You going to save us?" I grin at him.

He puffs out his chest. "I'll bring my Commando Xylex proton laser gun and rocket blaster. Bam-bam." His pointed index finger shoots at the ceiling of the car. "Commando Dylan Xylex saves the universe and the Ladies Kent from Zoidian aliens."

"You are my hero."

Joe leans forward. "You wouldn't know a Zoidian if he burped in your face." It isn't that funny but Sarah snarks through her nose and we all lose it.

Chapter Eight

Monday Night

At dinner, I tell Mom and Bella that Dylan is willing to stay overnight with us.

"We hired a security guard," Mom says. "He's going to sit in his car in front of the house, and every half hour, he'll check the back and side yards."

"What about the alarm system?" I ask. "Those guys aren't coming until tomorrow. Isn't that what you said?"

"Right."

"Well then—" I stare at Mom.

Bella picks it up. "I think we could use a man inside the house tonight, Charlotte." She passes Mom a bowl of green beans.

Mom gets it then and smiles. "Okay," she says. "But tell *the man* he'd better ask his parents."

"Great!" I say, and jump up to call Dylan. "Thanks, Bella."

"What about me?" Mom asks.

"You too," I say.

Dylan actually does bring the proton laser gun and rocket blaster and demonstrates the double-trigger action for all three of us in the kitchen. One trigger releases sparks and a zinging noise and the second trigger releases the rocket blaster with red and blue lights flaring. Dylan adds *chuff chuff* shooting noises with his mouth. We get the giggles watching him. Mom and Bella seem more relaxed. They are surprisingly relieved at the idea of having a guy stay with us—that and the security guy, Dwight Barnes, out in front.

"I feel safe," Bella says after the demonstration. "How long have you had this thing?" Even Bella knows that Commando Xylex TV programs haven't been popular for years. She holds the gun while Dylan replaces the rockets in the holders.

"I got it for Christmas five years ago." He looks up at her. "I've been waiting for the day when I could use it to protect you." He grins.

Bella lets out one of her horse laughs. Mom smiles across the table at me. They like him. Both of them. A swell of happiness builds in my throat like an aria and I cover my mouth with my fingers to squelch it.

We play Scrabble for an hour; Mom wins hands down. Bella makes up the sofa bed in Mom's study and goes upstairs. "Yell if you need help," she calls to Dylan.

"Can we watch TV together for a little while?" I ask. Mom looks down at what is now a bed in front of the TV. Caution lines appear on her forehead.

"In our jammies?" Dylan's look is pleading.

"Nice try, Commando," Mom says. "No jammies and only for an hour—and I'll be checking in every thirty seconds or so." She looks at us over her glasses.

"Guess we'll really watch TV then," Dylan says.

I elbow him. "Don't make jokes like that, or she'll send me upstairs."

"Thank you for reminding me of my duty, Lieutenant." He salutes me. "Ms. Kent, ma'am, I'll place this here weapon between your daughter and me to ensure her safety"—he glances at me—"and mine."

"One hour." Mom taps her watch. "Fresh cookies in the tin," she says on her way out.

"You get the milk and I'll get the cookies," I say to Dylan. I grab the whole tin. He carries a quart of milk and two glasses and waits for me to poof pillows at the back of the sofa. He lies against them, legs stretched out in front of him. I sit cross-legged, trying to pour milk without spilling.

He switches on the TV and surfs through the channels. "What do you want to watch—a *Friends* rerun, an *X-Files* rerun, or a Letterman rerun?"

I hand him a full glass of milk. We nod at each other. "*X-Files,*" we say at the same time.

He switches the channel. We've both seen the episode before but it's a good one. We eat cookies and watch until the commercial. He switches to mute and leans in for a kiss. He surrounds my bottom lip and—

"This is the first check," Mom's voice comes from the kitchen. I sit up straight and Dylan stuffs a whole cookie into his mouth. Milk spills. I laugh out loud.

Mom stands in the doorway. "Everything all right?"

"Fine." I'm snickering.

Dylan rolls his eyes and nods. "Good cookies," he says, but it comes out more like *foh gokies*.

"Bella uses pecans instead of walnuts. It makes all the difference," Mom says. "Okay then." And she disappears.

Dylan swallows several times. "I did *not* hear her!" He wipes his lips with his hands. "Will she be back?"

"For sure," I say. "But we have five minutes." I switch the light off next to the sofa so all that's left is the blue glow of the TV. This time I kiss him. He pulls me down. We are horizontal, and I try to forget that my mother would ground me forever if she found me horizontal with anyone, including Dylan. It seems like a stupid rule. I'm melting into his kisses. I have no sense of time with the TV muted.

The light glares on, and my mother stands above us. She gestures for me to move over and I scramble away from Dylan. She piles up a couple of pillows for herself and sits next to me. Dylan's mouth is shaped for a silent whistle. "Cozy," she says.

Mom leans across me and speaks to Dylan: "Now tell me again why you think high school students shouldn't read *The Scarlet Letter*?" Her smile is exaggerated. "What part of it don't you understand?" She looks at the TV. "Oh, *X-Files*. Oh, I like this. Turn on the sound."

Dylan's head falls back and he stares at the ceiling, his face the same color as Hawthorne's famous letter.

I'm so nervous I run out to pee. I laugh in the bathroom. I do that when I'm nervous: laugh and pee.

When I return I climb over Mom back to my seat next to Dylan. We grasp hands and dare to smile.

I don't see the end of *The X-Files*. I drift off to sleep in the blue light, hearing Scully's voice. When I wake up I hear different voices; the TV is turned off and the room is dark. It's Mom and Dylan whispering across me to each other: "He's coming toward the house from the garage—do you see him?"

"Who?" I say, startled.

They both shush me. "Keep your head down and pretend like you're sleeping," Dylan says.

"I was sleeping," I say.

Mom gasps. "Oh my lord."

"You see him?" Dylan asks.

"He's wearing a ski mask. Oh, oh—" She muffles her mouth with a pillow.

"Someone is out there?" It's a rhetorical question. Dylan's and Mom's voices are tight with tension. My heartbeat has doubled in the short time I've been awake.

"Are you sure it isn't that security guy?"

"He just came back here a few minutes ago, and he uses a flashlight. This guy's wearing a ski mask."

"Can you reach the phone?" Dylan asks.

I feel Mom grab the phone from the table next to the sofa and pull it to her ear. Her voice is low and controlled: "The line is dead."

Dylan gulps as if there isn't enough oxygen. "What about a cell phone?"

"Upstairs with Bella," Mom whispers. "I'm going out the front door and get Dwight." She slips out of bed and onto the floor, where she crawls toward the kitchen. "Don't do anything crazy," she calls softly. "He may have a gun."

My hands grow weak at the mention of a gun. This is not TV. I turn my head so I can see what they've already seen. There's only starlight. I can't see anything but the usual trees and bushes, shapes I know well. We are surrounded with floor-to-ceiling windows—this is the garden room. Now it's a fishbowl, although he shouldn't be able to see us any better than we can see him. It's dark. There's a movement by the sycamore tree. A dark figure moves away from the tree and closer to the house. I push my face into Dylan's arm. "He's coming," I say. My whole body shudders.

"Shhh." Dylan grasps my arm. "He doesn't know we're awake. He doesn't know we're even here."

"Can't he see us?"

"Your mother heard the garage door and we turned the TV off. If he saw us before, he thinks we've gone to bed. At least, that's what I'm betting on. He doesn't want us awake."

My words sound muffled against his arm. "How does he want us? Pickled?"

"He's got to be the same guy from last night. He ran away when he was chased." Dylan's breathing hard, so I know he's nervous, but his voice is calm. "My guess is he wants you all asleep when he enters the house." His arm goes across my back. "Shh. He's coming closer—stay still."

I'm paralyzed. There's a loud thump on the French door and I shudder. Dylan's arm tightens around me. "Glass cutter—" he whispers.

Oh God, keep us safe. Keep us safe. Please God, keep us safe.

What about the other people who asked for safety and didn't get it? That woman from the TV station in New York City. She was in the helicopter dropping out of the sky: "Oh Jesus, Jesus, save us. Hit the water! Hit the water!" Seconds later, she was dead.

Save *me*, Jesus. Me. Me. Me. Me and Dylan.

A shudder becomes a gag. Hasn't Mom reached the front door yet? I hope Dylan can't feel my body convulse. I hear the door handle being moved back and forth. There are deadbolts at the tops and bottoms of the doors, so he's going to need to cut a lot more glass than that. Jesus save us.

"Stay here." Dylan's arm slips away from me, away from the bed.

"Dylan—"

I twist and see him crouching and moving toward the end of the bed. The dark figure pulls the glass out of the pane. Then Dylan is up on his feet and roaring, "Get out

of here, or I'll kill you!" He lowers his voice. "Get out."
He points the proton laser gun with the rocket blasters
straight through the hole in the window at the figure,
who backs away, startled. Dylan pulls double triggers
and the gun explodes into lights and sparkles, and one of
the rockets hits the man in the shoulder. He grasps his
shoulder as he runs toward the back fence. I hear Mom
calling, "Dwight!"

I follow Dylan into the yard, where he takes off
through the back gate after the thief. He keeps blasting
away across the lawn, the gun *rat-a-tat-tat*ting although
the plastic rockets lie useless on the ground. Through all
the noise of the commando laser gun I can still hear
Dylan: *Chuff, chuff—chuff, chuff, chuff.*

I meet Mom and Dwight—useless security guard—
at the side of the house. "He must have timed my surveillance," Dwight Barnes says.

I want to laugh at his use of *surveillance.*

Bella joins us in her bathrobe. "Did he show up
again?"

Mom nods. "Dwight called the police, and they're on
their way."

Dylan, elation on his face, the gaudy proton laser gun
at his side, walks along the side lawn, puffing and grinning. "I just scared the crap out of myself," he says.

"Only professionals should go after perps," Dwight
says. *Perps?*

Mom puts her arm around Dylan. "You shouldn't have
done that. It was much too risky."

"You think?" He laughs. "You should have seen him run, though."

"Your parents are going to kill me when they hear about this," Mom says, but she strokes his arm.

"I don't really want to be Commando Xylex." He grins.

I stand next to him hugging myself. It isn't cold but I can't stop shivering. My teeth chatter. "You scared him off with a *toy,* a kid's toy. You're crazy."

He grins and nods. "Yeah, I think so." He lifts the proton laser gun. "Or maybe I was meant to be a super-hero."

"You think?" I bite back a smile.

"Geez, that was scary," he says.

"You've always been my hero," Bella says.

That should have been *my* line.

We are up until three with the police, who tell us that our phone line was cut. Dylan's parents, who come to see what's going on with all the cop-car lights flickering in front of our house, insist we stay at their place. "If he comes back, let it be to an empty house," Neil Madsen says. Mom and Bella don't say anything about what a bother we'd be but follow Ruth Madsen gratefully into the house. We sleep in the guest room on the second floor, which has two full-size beds in it. I lie next to Mom awake, listening to the night noises real and imagined. A thought comes to me that I haven't considered: Someone wants to kill us. He's not after Bella's antiques; if he were, wouldn't he wait until we were all out of the house? No, he comes when he knows we're home. That isn't a thief. That's a killer. A serial killer, maybe. Someone who kills women related to each other. The Generational Killer. That's what he'd be called. We'd be one of those unsolved crime cases on A&E and the same bad photos of Mom, Bella, and me would appear on the screen over and over again. I can hardly breathe, it makes so much sense there in the dark. I grab Mom's arm. "You awake?" I whisper.

Mom turns in the bed to face me. "Completely."

I stare into her eyes, not sure I want to form the question.

"What?" she whispers.

"Do you think this guy—the one tonight—is the same person who killed Maude?"

Her lips press together. "Maybe—I don't know. There seems to be a pattern forming."

"I'm scared."

She brings the blanket up around my neck and holds it there. "Yes." She tucks her hair behind her ear. "We're going to a hotel for a few days."

"I'm awake." Bella's voice fills the room. "We'll survive this just fine." She flicks on a bedside lamp and sits up. "We will," she says, thrusting a small fist into the air, "because we're survivors."

I want to believe her, but I can't really think of anything serious we're ever had to survive, except maybe the two-day power outage three years ago when we had an ice storm. Hardly a trial. We watched movies in heated theaters. All three of us gained weight on cheese nachos and Dove bars.

"We don't even know who we're fighting," I say.

"A coward," Bella says. "He kills a poor defenseless dog, and so far he's been scared off by a seventy-year-old man and a teenager with a toy laser gun."

I smile, but then I think about the wire tying Maude's paws together. Why? Only a psychopath would think of that. Someone without rational sense. My limbs grow weak with anxiety. "Maybe we should go to Europe right away," I say. Now, in this cowardly moment, it seems like an excellent idea.

"We can get a passport within a week," Mom says. Obviously she thinks so too.

Bella adjusts her pillows. "Sounds fine to me," she says. "It'll take a week to get my business in order. Judy will finally have some of that responsibility she thinks she's so ready for." She leans back on her elbows and realizes she's looking straight into a mirror on the closet door. "I look like an old woman." There's real surprise in her voice. "I've turned into a hag, a crone." She spreads her lips to reveal her teeth. "Are these veneers getting darker?"

Mom and I snigger, and it feels good. "You've been a witch ever since I've known you," I say.

Bella directs a stern glare my way and turns out the light. "You've got my DNA, girl," she says.

I want the light on. I lie on my side and heave a little

sigh. "I wish we had a man living with us," I say. I'm thinking of Daddy.

"We could hire one," Bella says. "In fact, we already have. Dwight!"

"Is he still out there?" I ask.

"I paid him for the whole night. So far, I haven't had my money's worth."

I lower my voice and try to imitate Dwight: *"Only professionals should go after perps."*

Mom and Bella convulse into laughter.

"Oh, Mirabelle." Mom sighs. "My Mira-cle. My Mira-bear."

Bella chimes in: "Mira–bug breath."

"Spiderwoman," I say.

I hear Bella turn over. "I give up." She yawns. "I can't compete with such a vicious young mind."

Mom and I spoon hug like we used to when I was young and skittish about night and its secrets. Mom hums the alto part of an old hymn: "Now the Day Is Over." I harmonize with her for a few minutes. I think I fall asleep smiling.

Chapter Nine

Tuesday

It's early morning when Mom, Bella, and I go home to shower and dress. Over cereal, they tell me that they will pack us up and when I get home from school we will move to a hotel downtown. Mom is skipping another day of school and even Bella the workaholic says she'll stay home to meet with the man from the security company. Unheard of.

"What if *he* comes again?" I ask.

"Well, I doubt we'll be seeing him in the middle of the day," Bella says.

"I want to stay home too," I say. "I can help pack."

Mom and Bella exchange glances. "Honey, go off and enjoy," Mom says. "The last week of school is too fun to miss. We'll be all done when you get home. I'll pack your bathing suit. The hotel has a large pool." Her voice is too enthusiastic and the pool sounds like a bribe.

"Well, that makes it all worth it," I say with more snarl than I intend.

Mom's shoulders sag. "Mira, please—"

"Okay!" I hold my hands up in surrender. "I'm going, I'm going."

Mom bends over the dishwasher. "I'll pick you up after school. Wait for me out in front."

"I can ride home with Dylan—"

"Not today. Wait for me." She looks up at me, her lips pressed together to make that serious face—that I-am-your-mother face.

"Whatever." I run upstairs to get my backpack and expect to see Maude following me, yipping at my heels. I think it'll be a while before I stop looking for her. I check my hair once more and hear Dylan's car horn honk. I grab my things and run down the stairs.

"Remember, out in front after school," Mom calls from the kitchen.

I slam the front door behind me. I don't even know why I'm annoyed.

In fact, school is fun. Mr. Sebastian brings his electric guitar to choir and we sing rock and roll instead of Bach chorales. He turns the volume way up and we're all shouting and waving our hands as Mr. Sebastian grinds his hips and plays his guitar. He's Elvis! Awesome. Why do teachers always show themselves the last week of school? I asked Mom this once and she said you can't be the students' friend or they'll walk all over you.

I know she's right. I think of Ms. Littleman, who flirts with the boys and lets them call her Carol. What a ho.

Dylan, Sarah, Joe, and I go out for Chinese at lunch and eat in the cemetery at Lizzie Borden's grave, our favorite shady spot. Elizabeth Borden, really, but we call her Lizzie. My fortune says I have big changes coming into my life. Sarah's says that she has a winning and bright personality. "Tell me something I don't know," she says, flicking the fortune into the wind. Joe's says he will be a big success in his employment. "Yeah, fast food loves me," he mutters. Dylan's fortune is that he will find love close by. He hesitates to read it and when he does, he blushes, which makes him look even cuter. He gets big razzes from Sarah and Joe. He gives his fortune to me. "Paste it in our book," he jokes, grinning, and Sarah and Joe howl imitations: "*Our* book. Paste it in *our* book."

I slip it into the pocket of my khakis and grin unabashedly. What can I say? He's darling.

In history, we play a game: Which dictator am I? Dr. Francis (the only teacher at our high school with a PhD—she never lets us forget it) pins pictures of dictators past and present on our backs, and we have to write the names of as many as possible. Then we're supposed to figure out who is on our backs by asking yes-or-no questions. It doesn't surprise me that Dr. Francis has actually managed to collect thirty pictures of dictators. She probably keeps a scrapbook of them. They're her paper dolls. We get candy kisses for every point we make.

Sarah wants to come home with me, and we wait on

the front steps along with other kids waiting for rides. "Where is she?" I say.

"Maybe she's out buying you an end-of-the-year present!" Sarah says. She gets up and dances back and forth on the steps. "You know what next year is, don't you?" She bobs back and forth on her feet. "It's our lucky junior year. We will never be happier than we are next year. We will never be prettier, or stronger, or more passionate. This is our year! Whooeee!" She howls at the sky. "Whooeee!"

Kids all around us turn, some smiling, some rolling their eyes.

"Women are most passionate at forty," I say. "I read that somewhere."

"Gross," Sarah says. "I am Sarah; hear me howl." She beats on her chest. "This is our year for L-I-F-E, for everything." She flings her arms out.

"How about maturity?" I say. I look north for Mom's Honda. I expected her to be waiting when we came out.

"I thumb my nose at maturity," Sarah says. "I lower my pants at it." She unzips.

"Stop," I say. "Geez, do you need meds or something? You're manic."

Big horse laugh. "Why are you so uptight? We're going to Europe!" She knocks into me.

"Sarah!" I'd rather visit my dad than see Europe with Sarah when she's in one of her hyper moods.

Lots of cars stop by to pick up kids, even a couple of Hondas. But none of them is Mom's Honda. I look at my watch. School has been out twenty minutes already.

Sarah notices. "She probably had to stop off for gas or buy a new thesaurus. That's it. She's lost her thesaurus."

I laugh then, because it rings true. "Let's start walking," I say. "If we see her, we'll flag her down." I turn toward the corner.

Sarah follows. "Maybe she's buying her own Commando Xylex proton laser gun and rocket blaster so she won't have to use a lecherous young man to guard her daughter. That's what *I'd* be doing."

"It's Dylan she needs to guard." I feel giddy. We both giggle. She hiccups convulsively and I laugh and snark through my nose. Sarah's knees buckle and we stand at the corner leaning into each other, laughing too loudly about absolutely nothing but our own silliness. It's exhilarating. We stop at the 7-Eleven for Dr Peppers for the walk home. Mom has either forgotten or found something more pressing to do.

We stop at Sarah's house long enough to drop her backpack inside the side door. Sarah insists we scissor-step to my house in an effort to stave off maturation. As if.

Our front door is ajar. "Hey!" I call. "Where were you?" I drop my backpack at the bottom of the stairs. "Mom? Bella?"

The silence grips us both. "Odd," Sarah whispers. A slice of sunlight cuts into the hallway from the kitchen and makes a glittering pattern on the wood floor. I turn toward it. Sarah and I know at the same time and gulp in air. Splattered blood dots the floor and wallpaper. "Blood," I say, but I'm already outside myself. I'm in a tunnel. A few more steps and I am almost at the door to the kitchen. A bloody hand mark mars the counter near the door.

Sarah grasps my arm with both hands and pulls back. "Don't," she cries. "Don't go in there." But I cannot be stopped and yank myself free. "Mom! Momma!" Again the voice comes from far away. Already I am two people. One watching the other do what she knows she must do. I am in the doorway and see it all. Bella lies faceup near the doorway, her body punctured with gashes in her abdomen, her chest, her throat. Her eyes wide with the surprise of the attack.

Mom lies on her side in the doorway to the study, her back toward me. Someone is screaming. Sarah, maybe. Maybe not. Someone is really screaming. Listen to that girl scream. I turn my mother over and I think she may be alive still. I think she may be alive. Mommy is alive. That girl thinks so. Who will stop that wailing girl? Do something useful, like clean up all that blood, you stupid cow. Gallons of it sprayed around the kitchen. Bloody gallons. Wipe it off your mommy's face with your T-shirt. Wipe it off her arms. Where is her shoe? Someone has stolen one of her shoes. Give her back her shoe. It's her shoe. Wipe her foot. I will wipe her foot with my hand and then wipe my hand on my jeans and wipe her legs and her feet. Stop that bloody screaming! You girls are going to get it if you don't stop.

She's on her knees kissing her mother on the face and neck and saying, "Please don't die, Mommy. Please don't. I love you, Mommy. Mommy?" Her mother groans softly, but the girl hears it like a gong, sees the blood burbling out of a hole in her mother's chest, and she remembers the thing, the thing to do. She pulls her own T-shirt off and wads it in a ball and holds it tightly against that hole. Stuff that bloody hole. Pressure. The girl leans over her mother. "Don't die. Don't die. Don't die."

That other girl, who is her friend, brings her own mother with her. The mother says a little prayer—*O God help us all*. The police are on the way, one of them says. The girl hears the sirens and holds the T-shirt on the hole in her mother's chest. The other mother lifts the first mother's legs up onto stacked pillows, and covers as much of her as she can with a blanket. All of this the girl sees from her peripheral vision. She never takes her eyes off her mother's face. If you keep things in your line of vision, they cannot disappear. This is a rule she has just made up and she thinks it's a very good rule. Then men come in without knocking and give her mother oxygen and an IV and two of them pull the girl away—it takes two of them—and they put her mother on a gurney and everyone looks sober and the girl yells that she must keep seeing her mother's face. She swings at them when they disagree. She swings hard, because she is young and strong and full of passion to save her mother and no one is going to tell her what to do. Do you hear me? Do you hear me?

Someone gives the girl a shot and she slumps down, down, catching a glimpse of her grandmother's open stare.

Chaos follows. Police cars, an ambulance, a fire engine, empty their foot soldiers into our house. I am moved around by people—mostly Mrs. Sullivan, whose fingers are cold when she grasps me around the shoulder and walks me into the living room to sit on the sofa. Sarah gives me another T-shirt to put on. I am drugged and find it hard to focus. Do I see them trying to revive Bella? Do I hear it, or do I imagine it, like some rerun of *Law & Order*? I already know what the result will be. It is not unlike a mathematical formula that is tried and true. She is dead beyond reviving. I saw it in her eyes. She is gone. Bella is gone to bigger and better mansions. Real estate heaven. "When I go . . . ," she used to say. Only I never believed she would go. I don't think she believed it herself.

Mrs. Sullivan holds me close and strokes my hair. I hear her heart beating. "Mom." I say it aloud. "I need my mom." Mommy.

"They're just getting ready to take Mrs. Kent to the hospital," a male voice says. I turn and see a uniformed man speaking not to me, but to Sarah's mother, who nods.

"I want to go with her," I say, standing just in time to see a filled body bag being rolled out through the front hall. It's a blow to my solar plexus and I sag back into the sofa. Sarah, who sits on the other side of her mother, wipes her splotched, wet face with the palms of her hands.

"I have to go to the hospital," I say, but I feel weighed down by gravity. By graveness.

"We'll follow the ambulance." Sarah's mother has her arm around me again and Sarah reaches across her mother's lap, her hand clutching my knee.

"Okay," I say. "Okay." I can't stop saying it. "Okay, after the ambulance, then we'll go. Okay."

Mrs. Sullivan nods.

When I see my mother on the gurney, her face is white as school paste, and there's a tube stuck in her mouth connected to some breathing apparatus. An IV is attached to her arm, which has angular gashes all along it. Both hands are bandaged. One of the paramedics presses a huge bloodstained cotton wrap against one side of her chest.

"Is she going to live?" I ask, standing. "She's going to be okay, isn't she?" I follow after the gurney.

"She's tough," says the guy. They're fast, and soon Mom is in the ambulance with its flashing lights and anxious wail.

"She's my mom." My voice is thin and dissipates into the warm May afternoon.

At the hospital we wait along with other visitors. The television high in a corner plays CNN, the reporters' voices low, their faces set against a now familiar Iraqi landscape. I look up distractedly but cannot follow the commentary. Mrs. Sullivan makes Sarah and me drink orange juice. I have almost forgotten how to swallow. Outside the window I see cars pass on the streets and marvel how anyone can be having a normal day on this of all days: the day my grandmother was murdered. The day my mother was almost murdered. Almost. She was not murdered. She was almost murdered. Let this be true, God.

Dylan and his parents show up. I can't stand to greet them. Neal and Ruth Madsen say how sorry they are about Bella and ask what they can do. I have no idea what the question means and stammer incoherently. Ruth Madsen hugs me. They sit with Sarah's mother, speaking in low voices.

Dylan sits with me. "I should have stayed," he whispers. "I should have stayed all day." He looks devastated.

I shake my head. "No," I say. You'd be dead now, I think. Or almost dead.

"I can't believe Bella is gone," he says.

I lean my forehead against his shoulder. "You smell so good," I say. A totally inappropriate thing to say. "I mean—" I don't know what I mean. He does smell of Old Spice, but so what? "It helps," I say.

"Like waffles on a Saturday morning?" he asks.

"Something like that, yes."

"I'm going to miss Bella's waffles." He takes my hand.

Dr. Sullivan arrives soon after the Madsens with Josh in tow. "Dad says we can eat at the hospital today," Josh says to Sarah. When her dad puts his arm around her, she weeps into his sleeve.

I haven't cried. Kent women don't cry. That's what

Bella says. *Said.* Bella is past tense. Should I be crying now? I hear my mother's voice: "Do I dare to eat a peach?" She quotes that T. S. Eliot line when I ask silly questions. Mom quotes poets. Mom is still present tense. I cross my fingers.

We have dinner in the hospital's cafeteria after a nurse tells us that Mom is in surgery and that it will likely take several hours.

"Will she be okay?" I ask.

The nurse is noncommittal. "I hope so," she says.

Dr. Sullivan is more positive. "Your mother is young and healthy. Her odds are very good." He, like the rest of us, plays with his lasagna. He winks at me for added comfort. I know he's speaking as a friend and not as a doctor.

Mom comes out of surgery about ten that night. I am allowed into the ICU. Dr. Sullivan comes with me. I'm not prepared for what I see: my mother, mangled and broken, breathing with the help of a respirator, bandaged around her chest, her hands, tubes everywhere, her face swollen and bruised. I hold on to one arm and stare down. Dr. Sullivan explains her injuries in a low, steady voice: something about her spleen, barely missing an important artery, a punctured lung, defensive wounds. I swallow down my anxiety again and again and again. "I want to stay with her," I say.

I expect some kind of adult reply, some huffing and puffing about how that's not a good idea, but he surprises me: "I think you should." He points at a chair in the corner. "This turns into a bed. I'll have the nurse get you a pillow and a blanket."

"Thank you." I look up at him.

He nods, opens his mouth—to give advice maybe—but changes his mind. He shrugs, pats my shoulder, and leaves.

Dylan pokes his head inside the door. "I'm going to stay in the waiting room tonight, so if you get lonely, I'll be across the hall." He blanches when he sees Mom. "Geez." It catches in his throat. He looks. "You okay?"

I nod. "You don't have to stay."

"I know." There's a grim smile and he's gone.

Sarah stands at the door. "We can only come in one at a time." She moves to the other side of the bed from me, her fingertips touching Mom's fingertips. The oxygen pump makes a hissing sound and a monitor in the corner beeps monotonously. "There's going to be a policeman outside the door," Sarah says. "They're not taking any chances now."

I fill in the rest: now that one person has already died. I wonder where Bella is now. Does she know who did this? Could she tell us if she were here? It doesn't matter anymore. Still—

"I have to go home, but I'll be back in the morning, so Dylan can go home and shower. We'll both be around tomorrow."

"School's not over," I say.

"It is for us," she says. "Will you call if your mom comes to? We all want to know. It doesn't matter if it's the middle of the night."

"I will," I say. "Thanks. And thank your parents—I forgot to."

She comes around the bed and hugs me. "I'm so sorry," she says. "I'm really so sorry."

I don't know what to say. "See ya" is all that comes to mind.

Then I'm alone. I sit in the chair, my arms folded tightly in front of me. "Don't let her die—" I say aloud. Is it a prayer? "Please don't let her die." I hope someone powerful is listening.

I dream I am following my mother uphill and call her name. I'm exhausted from the climb and my voice is thin and raspy. I try harder but she makes her way lightly; a pastel veil around her neck blows romantically behind her, as does her hair, like in those nineteenth-century Victorian paintings that she despises. Smarmy, she says. I try to call more loudly so she'll stop, but my voice dissipates as soon as it comes from my lips. When she reaches the top of the hill she turns and looks down at me. At first she smiles, glad to have me there, but then she grows increasingly anxious, until her mouth becomes an oval, releasing a loud surround-sound scream. My mother's scream is killing me. I'm dying.

A monitor is beeping when I awake. My heart pounds and I am sweaty with fear. Sweaty with the touch of the Naugahyde chair-bed. Sweaty with disorientation. I draw the single blanket around my face and breathe deeply into its woven texture. A nurse pops in and checks my mother. "Oops, this oxygen clip fell off her finger," she tells me. She pushes a button that stops the beep. "Her color is a bit better," she says. "She's very pretty."

My heart is booming under the blanket. I nod at her.

"You must look like your dad," she says. Has she just told me I'm ugly?

"All that red hair—" She smiles, and I realize she means well.

She leaves the room. I'm afraid of the dream, afraid of my mother's screaming. I get up and wrap the blanket around my shoulders. The light in the hall makes me squint. A policeman sits in a chair reading a magazine a few steps from Mom's room, a leather holster with a gun at his side. I cross the hall into the waiting room. An older woman is curled up on a couch at the other end of the room, newspapers strewn on the floor beneath her.

Dylan lies on his back on a sofa to my right, a blanket bunched up around his neck. I stand over him trying to match my breathing to his. Beautiful. He is beautiful. Can you say that about a boy? He'd be embarrassed to know I thought so. I push his nose lightly with my index finger. "Anybody home?"

He turns on his side, swallows, and swats the air above his face. I run my finger across his forehead.

His head jerks up, eyes open—

I manage a smile. "I had a bad dream," I say.

He looks around, confused, then runs a hand over his face. He pats the seat next to him. His feet hit the floor and I sit down. He blinks several times, trying to wake up.

"Sorry I woke you," I say. It's a huge lie.

"No," he says, grabbing my arm. "That's why I'm here, so you can wake me up—is your mother okay?"

"She's the same. I dreamed she was screaming. It filled my head. She was standing on a hill—"

"Was she mad?"

"No, she was afraid."

"Of you?"

"No." I try to think. "Of someone behind me."

He waits for me to tell him who. "I can't remember." Another lie. I shake my head. "I just remember fear. It was surreal."

"It's an anxiety dream. They're the worst," he says. He stands and slides a love seat close to the sofa. "Here, put up your feet and I'll put mine up." He reaches over to fix my blanket and pulls up his own. We lean into each other. "You need a lullaby," he says. He must see the skepticism on my face. "I'm the only one in the family who can get my niece, Daisy, to sleep when she's wound up," he says as proof of his abilities. "Ready?"

My head rests against his shoulder. "Sing away, Uncle Dylan."

He hums a starting pitch for himself and sings in a clear baritone voice:

> *"How doth the little crocodile*
> *Improve his shining tail,*
> *And pour the waters of the Nile*
> *On every golden scale!*
> *How cheerfully he seems to grin,*
> *How neatly spreads his claws,*

And welcomes little fishes in,
With gently smiling jaws!"

Dylan smiles a crocodile grin.

I cover my laugh with the blanket. "That puts Daisy to sleep?"

"The rockabye rhythm does. She doesn't understand the words yet."

"A good thing," I say.

We sing it together a couple of times and he adds harmony. Our voices blend. "We can take it on the road," he says. "We'll be the Crocodiles." His lips press against my hair and I'm not afraid anymore. I feel happy, but it doesn't seem right. How can I be happy and so utterly sad at the same time? How can I be this happy when Bella is dead, and Maude is dead, and Mom is half dead?

"Sing some more," I say, tears falling.

Kent women do cry.

I wake up before it's light. Dylan's head rests on the back of the sofa and he snores gently. I slip back into Mom's room. When the nurse comes in, I ask, "Is she okay?"

The nurse says Mom's vital signs have been strong all night. "Now she just needs to wake up. That will make us all feel better."

When the nurse is gone, I bend over Mom. "Wake up, Mom. You've got to wake up."

Her eyes flutter briefly and close again. I'm elated. "Mom, that was good. Try it again." Nothing. Still, I feel more confident and fall asleep in the chair. I dream again of Daddy. This time he waits for me at the airport, but I can't get in. I can see him through the plate glass window, but he doesn't see me. I knock and yell, and make large gestures with my arms, but he never looks toward the glass. I wake up with Sarah standing over me. "What day is it?" I ask.

"Wednesday," she says. She is all cleaned up and crisp looking.

I sigh with relief. "I dreamed I missed my dad at the airport."

"You're not still going, are you?"

"I don't know," I say. And that's the truth. "I can't leave now, but I also need Daddy right now."

She breathes deeply. "Are you ready for some breakfast? Dylan's taking you to his house to eat, and then you can shower and change your clothes and come back."

I nod and stand up. "You going to stay with her?" I nod at Mom.

"Yes, and my mom is coming in a little while. There will be people here all day to be with you." She smoothes Mom's sheets.

"Maybe I should wait until the doctor comes." I feel hesitant about leaving. "She fluttered her eyes—"

"That's a good sign," Sarah says. "I'll tell the doctor if he comes while you're gone. My dad is going to speak with him too. Go on, now. You look like a wreck."

In Dylan's car on the way home, I notice blood on my arms. I run my fingers over it. "Tonight my dad comes," I say.

"I wondered if you were still planning to go." He says this cautiously.

"Do you think he could have attacked them?" I ask. "They changed their names and moved across the country. My mom said that some people should never marry. She meant my dad."

Dylan bites his lip and weighs his answer. "I think you have to consider him," he finally says.

I know he's right. It makes me tired.

We drive by my house, and I see yellow police tape across the front door. "I need some clothes," I say.

"Sarah brought some of her things. You can't go in there. The detective said they'll probably be done this afternoon. You can get some clothes then."

I feel a little better after breakfast, a shower, and clean clothes. The day is filled with neighbors coming to give condolences or to sit with Mom for a while. Judge and Eileen Dayton bring me lunch. Mom flutters her eyes more often but can't seem to keep them open. Her doctor is optimistic and the nurse tells us to keep talking to her, that we don't know what she can hear. A one-sided conversation is exhausting, but I keep trying.

In the afternoon I decide that I will go to the airport to meet my father. If I see him, I will know everything. I will know. And besides, what could Daddy do in a crowded airport? It's the little album with his watercolors that puts him into the plus column. Now that I've made up my mind, I don't really want Dylan to come with me. I don't want to hear his adultlike cautions anymore. I don't want to have to discuss it with him all the way to the airport. I need support right now, not arguments.

I sit with Mom most of the afternoon so that Dylan and his mother can take my place later. It turns out just as I orchestrate it. At six, I go out and say I need to get some dinner and ask Sarah if she wants to go down to the cafeteria with me. "Maybe we can get a shake somewhere too," I say.

Mrs. Madsen and Dylan have already had dinner and they decide to take turns sitting with Mom. Dylan goes first. "Remember to talk to her," I say. "Or you could sing to her."

Dylan smirks. "My singing puts people to sleep," he says. "We want her to wake up." I can tell he's forgotten about my dad. Maybe it's because I truly am tired and don't look as if I'm going on any kind of adventure. When he disappears into the ICU, I grab Sarah. "Let's go," I say.

"Are you sure you should go now? I mean there's a lot going on here." She looks toward Mom's room and then back to me.

"Yeah, there's a lot going on. I need family around me. I need a father more now than ever." I head toward the elevators. Sarah follows.

We meet her parents at the elevator doors and they tell us to go somewhere outside the hospital to eat. Dr.

Sullivan hands Sarah some money. "Get something good, and then take Mira for a ride. She needs to be out of this place for a while."

I smile at him. "Thanks," I say.

"Be careful," Mrs. Sullivan says, almost as if she knows what we're doing.

"I'm an excellent driver," Sarah says, sounding like *Rain Man*.

"Be careful anyway," she says.

Then we're in the elevator and the doors close. I take a deep breath. "We're on our way," I say. "I was afraid Dylan would remember and spoil everything."

"He's a little jealous, I think," Sarah says. "Your dad is a lot of competition."

"That's silly," I say, but I remember the dream where Dylan and Dad were interchangeable and I can't help shuddering.

Chapter Ten

Wednesday

We have to drive the circular route in and out of the airport twice, because Sarah is in the wrong lane for the
short-term parking. She is a new driver and nervous
about changing lanes in traffic. I'm pretty sure I'm doing the right thing by meeting Daddy. I'll know when I
see him. I'll know. And I need all the help I can get.
When he learns about everything that has happened,
he'll want to stay and take care of things. He'll want to
help. If Mom and he had been together in the first place
this wouldn't have happened. No one would bother a
house with a man in it. It's because we were three women
alone that we were victimized. I am sure of this. Stalked,
maybe. I heard a detective mention that possibility.
"Three for the price of one" is what he said. He didn't
know I was listening. Could Daddy be stalking us? I've
thought of this before. Why would someone who's never

even had a parking ticket suddenly begin killing people? It makes no sense. No sense at all.

Sarah parks in outer darkness. "Can't we get any closer?" I ask.

"My dad says it's less likely that people will hit you if you park away from other cars." We get out and she checks twice to make sure the car is locked. Even though we have plenty of time, we run from the parking lot into the airport and onto the escalator going down to the baggage claim area.

"Remember, we're not going anywhere with him," Sarah says. "You promised me." She bites her thumbnail, which I haven't seen her do since middle school.

"How many times do I have to promise?" Her anxiety irritates me. I step off the escalator and look around. No redheads except me.

Sarah follows me to a row of seats. "I'm afraid you'll change your mind, is all; that you'll decide having dinner in the city with him is just dandy, and I don't think it's a good idea." We sit down. I hug Daddy's photograph album to my chest. Sarah had hidden it in her glove compartment.

Sarah fidgets. "I wish we'd told my parents we were coming down here."

"Like they would let us come if we did!"

"We could have said we wanted to watch the planes." Sarah bites a nail.

"We haven't done that since we were twelve!" Her

nervous biting irritates me. "My gosh, if you're so worried, then go home. You're spoiling the whole thing for me." I give her the look. "You act like he's some kind of degenerate. I'm sick of it."

Sarah pouts. "Somebody has to be cautious," she hisses.

"I won't leave the airport. Pinky bloody promise."

"Good enough." She slumps in her seat.

I check out a fresh group of passengers coming down the escalator from the gates and watch them disperse around the luggage carousel.

"You have to be Mira," a male voice says.

My head swivels. Sarah straightens. He's handsome. My dad is handsome and I see parts of myself in his face. He's my dad and I was right to come. He looks wonderful.

"Daddy," I say. I wish I had taken more time to dress for this. I am rumpled and he is so polished.

He's carrying a pup that looks like Maude when she was a baby. "I brought you a present," he says, lifting his arm slightly, "and if she pees on this jacket, I'll never forgive her."

His smile disarms me. I stand and take the dog from him, but even when she licks my face my attention is fully focused on my father's face. "Oh, thank you," I say. Inside, I am rejoicing: I was right to come. I was right!

"I'm Sarah." Sarah stands and stretches out her hand. "I've been Mira's best friend since we were five. I can fill you in on the good stuff."

They shake hands. "Nice to meet you, Sarah." He gives her only a brief glance. She is not the one he has come to see.

"I brought this album you made. I *think* you made it." I almost drop it, because the puppy squirms in my arms.

Sarah takes the dog and walks a few steps away to give us a little privacy.

"You have this?" He opens it up. "Amazing." He browses through it.

I want to hug him, but I don't dare. He seems too formal to hug. "I've missed you so much," I say instead.

He likes this and takes my hand in both of his. "And I've missed you." He pats my hand. "This is a momentous occasion."

I nod, giddy with happiness and secure enough to say, "I'm sure we can talk Mom into letting us see each other sometimes."

He stiffens. "Your mother—" There's no inflection. A muscle in his cheek knots up. "How is your mother?"

I forget he doesn't know. I stammer—what to tell him? "She's—she's fine."

Sarah looks up at me.

Should I say something about Bella? About the hospital? It's too much. It's too much to organize into speech.

Daddy's eyes gaze into the distance beyond my head. He's remembering her. "That's good," he says. "I'm glad she's doing well."

Sarah approaches with the jittery pup. "I think this puppy needs to pee. We'd better move outside," she says.

I turn toward the door, but Daddy grasps my arm. "Would you mind taking her, Sarah, so Mira and I can talk?" He looks at his watch. "I have to be back at the gate in under an hour."

Sarah looks down at the dog and then at Daddy and me. "I think she can wait a few minutes." She turns her back on us and walks a few steps away.

She annoys my dad. His lips are pressed together for control. She annoys me too. "For heaven's sake," I say. "We don't need a guard. Lighten up."

Sarah turns, a surprised look on her face. It's an act. I know Sarah.

Daddy's jaw relaxes. "She's right," he says to me. "I'm the one who told you to bring a friend along and she's doing exactly what she's supposed to be doing— protecting you."

"But I don't need protection," I say. I want him to like me. I want things to go smoothly.

"You can never be entirely sure of that, and Sarah is smart enough to know that. In fact, aren't young girls often stolen from their neighborhoods with the promise of puppies and kittens?" Dad's voice is light now, and even Sarah smiles. I smile too.

"Did you bring a kitten too?" she teases.

"That would be too much of a good thing," he says with a half smile.

"Anyway," I say, "we're in the airport; what could happen?" I sound defensive. I wish I had come alone.

Sarah shifts the puppy to the other shoulder. "Okay,

then," she says. "I think there are a few places to eat upstairs. Maybe you'd like to go up and sit at a table. I'll take the dog for a walk and wait for you down here, if you like."

"Thank you," I gush. I know it's against her better judgment.

"I'll be around." She looks at Daddy and raises her eyebrows.

Daddy nods at her. "I'm on my guard," he says. He takes my arm and directs me toward the escalator. It doesn't take long to realize that all the places to eat are on the other side of the security gate. Daddy shakes his head. "This is a smaller airport than I remembered." He glances at his watch again. "Well, maybe this is all the time we get, Mira."

Is he leaving? Now? It feels as if everybody in my life is moving out of reach.

"No!" I cling to his arm. "We could just sit down and talk for a while," I say. "We don't need to eat or anything." I search the long corridors for a bench. "Come on, we'll go back downstairs. There are seats there."

He's thinking of alternatives. He's so elegant. He doesn't like me that much. He's disappointed. He doesn't care anymore. If he goes now, maybe I'll never see him again. "Please," I beg, pulling on his arm.

Then he smiles. "Of course," he says. "We can sit downstairs."

From the escalator I see Sarah coming through the automatic doors with the puppy wriggling in her arms.

"I like the dog," I say. "I've really missed Maude. She always slept on top of my bed. Mom called her the little sister. Silly, huh? Anyway, I'm glad you brought her. Maybe I'll name her Maude the Second. What do you think? Or Zoe? I like that name. I always wanted to have a name that started with Z." I'm a talking head. A motormouth. But nothing I say is of any consequence. "She'll always remind me of you, Daddy." I hear myself say it, but I don't believe it. It's like *We'll always have Paris.* I sound ridiculous.

"I'm glad you're pleased," he says. "That's what I hoped for." He glances at his watch again.

"You have time, don't you? You said almost an hour?" My voice squeaks like one of those singing chipmunks. Any second now, he'll yawn.

"You back already?" Sarah calls when she sees us.

"The restaurants are all on the other side of security," I say. "I can't get in without a ticket."

A man and a woman in matching leather jackets stop to see the dog and talk baby talk to it. Then a little girl breaks loose from her mother and wants to pet it. The dog is a novelty.

"Why don't we go out to your car," Daddy says to me. "I'll walk you girls out, we'll leave the dog there, and then you can walk me back, and by then it'll be boarding time."

"It's my car, actually," Sarah says. "But that would be great. It's like holding a small tornado."

"I'll take her," I say. The dog licks my face and I laugh.

Sarah leads the way up the escalator. She pulls the parking ticket out of her pocket.

"Let me pay the parking for you," my dad says, and takes the ticket from her hand.

"Oh, thanks," Sarah says.

We stop at the ticket office just before we go out to the parking lot and Daddy pays. He hands the stamped ticket back to Sarah.

"So have you always lived in Texas?" she asks my dad as we push through the doors.

I see the tiny knot about his jaw again. "No, only about thirteen years," he says.

"Since you and Mom divorced," I say.

"Since *she* left *me.*"

Sarah clears her throat. "Where did you grow up?" she asks. We wait at the crosswalk for a couple of airport buses to pass. "Mira wants to know everything about you," she says.

"And you are her mouthpiece?" The edges of his lips curve up.

"Yes, because I'm a genius and she's only gifted. My verbal scores are higher."

"So are Chatty Kathy's," I say. I glance at Daddy to see if he thinks I'm obnoxious, but he smiles. I made him smile. That's a good sign. I breathe easier. "Actually, she really is a genius." I can be generous now. "Her IQ is above one seventy."

"Well, only a little—" Sarah finds an iota of modesty.

"How is your grandmother?" Daddy changes the

subject. "I used to work for her, you know. She taught me the real estate business."

I have to cough before I can speak. "Fine," I say too quickly. My heart skips a beat and I feel my face flush. I pretend to fuss with the dog. "She's fine." I don't look at Sarah. I don't want to talk about it.

"She makes the best waffles in the universe," Sarah says. She spots her car.

"I remember them," he says. "Do you like to cook?" I see the red roof of Sarah's car at the end of the row. The time with my dad is more than half over.

"Not really," I say. "Mom and Bella both cook so well that I've never—"

"I don't like to cook either," he says.

I smile at him. We're alike, then, in some way. We have this negative thing in common, this noncooking gene.

"My favorite flavor is chocolate," I say.

He looks back and forth across the parking lot. "Me too," he says.

Sarah pulls her keys out of her pocket. "Here's my car." She unlocks and opens the back door. I bend and set the dog on the backseat and hurry to shut the door. The puppy scrambles around, falling back when she tries to get up to look out the window. She yips in a high voice. Both Sarah and I press our faces against the glass and coo at the dog. "How cute," we say, and "Poor puppy," and "I think she's a Zoe—"

I trip on my sandal when I am yanked by the elbow.

His grasp—Daddy's grasp—sends an electric shock through my funny bone. I let out a yelp, or is it the dog? I cannot process fast enough what is happening. It plays clip by clip: Sarah's head swivels and jolts at an odd angle when she sees my dad holding a gun. I see it at the same time. It's heavier looking than I would expect from a play gun. And it doesn't have that orange circle painted around the rim of the nozzle.

Sarah's mouth opens with "What—" but then he, my daddy, the man, thrusts his gun into her chest so hard it literally knocks the wind out of her. She sags against the car, her face grays, and her eyes bulge in alarm. He takes the parking ticket out of her hand and slips it into his pocket. My arm is nearly torn out of the socket. "Open the briefcase," he says to me. It is leaning against the back tire. He grips my arm as I unzip the leather bag. "Take out the cuffs!"

This isn't real, is it? I can't find the cuffs immediately and he yanks my arm behind my back at an impossible angle. I yelp.

"The cuffs," he hisses. "And shut your mouth."

I pull out the cuffs and he forces me to handcuff Sarah's hands behind her back. He holds the gun against Sarah's side, digging it in hard to make his point.

Sarah winces and groans.

"I'm sorry," I whisper. "I'm so sorry." I catch a glance of a family getting into a car but they are clear across the parking lot. How can it be so empty?

The dog is yipping and dancing in the backseat.

Daddy has me take a roll of duct tape out of his brief-case. "Tape her mouth shut." It is hard to imagine that he could ever have made that voice so charming.

"Oh, please don't," Sarah says. "I can't breathe through my nose—I'm a mouth breather, and—"

He hits her across the face with the gun. It makes a ter-rible thwacking sound. She groans. We are both crying silently. I break a strip of tape off with my teeth and tape her mouth. I break off a second piece at his insistence and tape her mouth again. I try to do it loosely, so she can breathe. Sarah and I look at each other and I know we are thinking the same thing: He will kill us.

"Get her in the trunk," he says to me. Sarah's eyes widen. I hesitate. Please, not in the trunk.

"Do it!" He shoves me into Sarah, who hits her head against the lid of the trunk and shuts her eyes against the pain. I help her sit in the trunk and then she lays her head down and I lift her legs in. I am barely out of the way before the demon daddy—my flesh and blood—slams down the lid of the trunk.

"In the car," he says to me. The point of the gun is pressed into my side. I sit in the passenger seat and he pulls another pair of handcuffs out of his briefcase and handcuffs my hands behind my back. It's torture. He tapes my ankles together. He is halfway into the car from the passenger side when he yanks my head back by the hair. "No funny tricks," he says, "or you're both dead. You understand?"

I am crying and cannot talk. He yanks my hair hard. "You understand?"

"Yes," I sob.

Then he does something no one has ever done to me before: he slaps me hard across the face. It stings and rocks my head. I cry out and he does it again. "You may have red hair but you're just like your mother." He shuts the door and walks around the front of the car.

The dog yaps behind me and tries without success to leap between the two front bucket seats. The back door on the other side opens; the pup's sharp yelps are helpless, but then there is silence. I turn my head to see the man—I can't think of him as Daddy anymore—holding the dog by its throat and yanking it out of the car. The door shuts. When he gets into the front seat, the dog is gone. We back out of the parking space and I feel the bump under the back tire and then the front tire. He has driven over the pup.

Pain, misery, and panic collide to bring on a black hopelessness. *He will kill us all: Bella, Maude, Mom, Sarah, me, and anyone else who stands in his way. He will kill us.* A terrible weakness in every muscle makes me nauseous. I want to throw up. I want it to be over.

Pull yourself together, Red, Red, Red. Bella's voice shouts inside my head. *Breathe, honey, just breathe slowly, and watch for your chance.* How will I know my chance?

We drive through the parking lot and approach the tollbooth. "Keep your mouth shut or I'll kill the parking attendant," the man says. I believe him.

The driver's window glides down and since he prepaid in the airport, he simply hands the ticket to the attendant and we're off. He accelerates down the airport exit road. He turns the radio on. The announcer says that in honor of spring, he'll play "Spring" from Vivaldi's *Four Seasons* before the news from the BBC. It must be close to eight o'clock. It is another perfect spring evening. The light is just beginning to turn golden, but it won't turn dark for another half hour. It is a warm day and I wonder how Sarah is faring in the trunk. Will the others at the hospital wonder why she and I are out so long? We've been gone a couple of hours.

After the news, the radio plays the Wednesday night opera, *The Barber of Seville*. I always liked this one when Bella played her CD. But he begins humming along with it, ruining it. After a minute, he switches it off. "Listen carefully," he says to me. "We're going to the hospital to see your mother. You will introduce me to your neighbors, who, I'm sure, are gathered around to succor the poor woman." He's enjoying this. "You will tell them that you called me and asked me to come, because you felt"—he turns and smiles at me—"alone? Yes, you were lonely." He smiles to himself now. "You without a grandmother—that was a flattering picture of her in the *Tribune* this morning—and your mother in a coma. So sad. Really so very sad."

We're going to the hospital?

"Are you listening?" he asks, his voice soft.

"Yes," I say.

"Good girl," he says. "Because you're going to have to do exactly as I say, or I'll kill you and a few of your friends." The car comes to a stop and makes a turn. "I know where that boyfriend of yours lives. I know which bedroom he sleeps in."

I swallow down the growing hysteria.

"And I have a real gun, not some silly toy." He sneers. "Although I prefer knives."

I shiver. He prefers knives? Dear Jesus, help us all.

"I've been looking for your mother and you for thirteen years, and then you call me right out of the blue looking for your long-lost daddy. It was like Christmas seeing 'Bella Kent' on the caller ID." His hand makes a flourish. "Of course, I didn't recognize the name Kent, but how many Bellas are there in this world? I knew it was you. What a dear you were to call." He pushes my shoulder as if this is a little joke between us. "All I had to do was look in the real estate section of the phone book and there she was." He leans close to me. "There all three of you were! Thought you could leave me and I'd forget about it?" His voice is feverish. "I'm the one who decides when you can go. Me!"

I am sick with guilt. I might as well have killed Bella myself.

"Think how surprised your mother will be to see me again." He lets out a smug laugh. "Twice in one week!"

When we get close to the university he turns into my neighborhood and stops in front of our house. "I assume you know the garage code," he says.

I tell him.

He gets out of the car, opens the garage door, and disappears into the house. Soon he's back in the garage; he gets into Bella's Mercedes and backs it onto the street.

I look around the block, hoping that someone is out, that someone is watching, but the street is quiet. Soon he's back behind the wheel, and he drives Sarah's car into the garage.

"Now." His mouth is close to my ear. "I'm going to release your hands and feet and we're going to drive to the hospital in Bella's car." He looks behind us. "Any funny business and you'll end up dead. That would be a shame. I look at your hair and it's like I'm looking at myself." He runs his hand through my hair and I shudder. "Beautiful," he says. Then he gets out of the car and comes around to my side. He takes the tape off my feet and unlocks the handcuffs.

I falter. "What about Sarah? They'll wonder where she is. They know I went with Sarah—"

His face darkens and he holds up an index finger. "I'm sure you can come up with something sufficiently believable. You'll have to. Everything depends on it." He takes my hand. "Look happy, now. Look happy that you've got your daddy with you."

He punches in the garage code and the door closes. We get into the Mercedes and head for the hospital. While he drives he pulls a towelette out of his pocket and hands it to me. "Better wipe your face," he says. "You look a little battered."

I do what he says.

When we move through the revolving doors of the hospital I see the sign for the first time: THIS IS A PLACE OF HEALING. PLEASE LEAVE YOUR FIREARMS AT HOME. Has that always been there? How could I have missed it? My father snorts when he sees it. I lead him to the elevator and push the fourth-floor button. A nurse gets on the elevator with us. She looks at the two of us and says, "You have to be father and daughter."

"Family curse," my father says.

I give a half smile and nod. Family curse indeed.

Dylan's and Sarah's mothers are in the waiting room. "Hi," I say with as much energy as I can muster.

They look surprised. "She's still out of it, but awake," Ruth Madsen says.

"She woke up? That's great news," I say.

Mrs. Madsen smiles and nods.

Sarah's mom says, "Dylan's in there singing to her." She looks back and forth between me and my father.

"Oh, I'm sorry—this is my father, Paul Weissmann. He's from Dallas. I called and asked him to come last night."

He shakes their hands and then puts his arm paternally around my shoulder.

"How nice of you to come," Sarah's mother says, looking at him carefully. "Where's Sarah?" she asks.

"Oh, she dropped us off at my house so we could use Bella's car. She said she had to go see Joe for a minute."

"I thought Joe was on vacation."

"Not until the weekend after school is out," I say. I'm talking way too fast.

"So the two of you went to the airport to get your dad?" she asks.

"I wanted it to be a surprise," I say. It sounds stupid even to me.

"Well, it's wonderful that you can have a family member here," Ruth Madsen says. "You'll want to go in. I'm sure your mother is eager to see you."

My heart picks up speed as we move toward the room. Demon man still has his arm around my shoulder, as if fathers and daughters go everywhere joined at the hip.

The policeman near the door nods at me. "This is my dad," I tell him. He smiles.

I stick my head in the door. "Hey," I say.

Dylan, who is sitting close to the bed, looks up. "Hey, you." He sees my dad and his eyebrows shoot up.

"My dad," I say.

Dylan glances at Mom, whose eyes are closed, pushes his chair back and stands up. He puts his hand out to my father, and they shake. "Nice to finally meet you."

I can tell he's impressed with Daddy.

"She was awake for about ten minutes," Dylan adds. "I told her you'd be back soon. Everyone's saying she's going to get well."

"That's good," I say.

"It's better than good," Dylan says. "You okay?" His eyes narrow for a closer look at me.

My father's grip on my shoulder tightens. "Me? I'm great. Probably I'm a little overstimulated." I force a grin.

"You think?" Dylan smiles at us.

"She needs a good night's sleep," my father says in his fake, soothing voice.

"I'm just glad to have my dad with me," I say, patting my father's hand. We look at each other and smile. My insides are clawing.

"I'll let you have your family reunion." Dylan turns away.

"Dylan," I call, my eyebrows raised as high as I can stretch them. *I'm different. Notice me.*

"Yeah?" He turns back.

Daddy grips my elbow tightly.

"Oh—nothing, I'll see you later."

I go over and sit next to the bed and bury my face in Mom's arm. "Mommy," I can't help saying. "Mommy, I'm sorry."

Mom's face remains placid.

My father stands over her on the other side of the bed. "She looks bad," he says. He plays with an IV, rolling it between his fingers. "So much equipment just to keep one person alive."

Mom's eyes flutter open. She sees me and her lips curve up slightly. She knows me. "Mom," I say. "You're awake." I hover above her face. I don't want her to see my father. "I'm so glad you're awake."

"We're both glad you're awake." The demon father brings his face close to Mom's. "Charlotte," he says. "I'm back."

Mom's eyes widen into panic. She turns her face away from him. On the monitor above her head, her heart rate shoots up. I'm scared. He's going to kill her. I do the only thing I can think of and slip the oxygen monitor off her finger. Immediately a loud buzzing begins.

My father doesn't miss a beat. He squeezes her face in his hand. "I hope I'm not making you nervous," he whispers in her ear.

"Please don't," I say, and reach for his arm, but he swings at me from across the bed.

He points a finger at me. "You cannot keep me from doing the inevitable." His face glowers in the half-light.

Gail, the night nurse, appears. "What's happening?" she says, looking at the monitors. "You two need to leave," she says. "I need to get her settled down." She places the oxygen monitor back on Mom's index finger.

Mom's head moves back and forth, her eyes bulging with terror. Gail continues, "There should only be one person in here—"

"I know, but my father wanted to see her."

Gail doesn't hear me anymore. "What is it, Charlotte? Where's all this anxiety coming from?" She strokes Mom's head and then starts looking for irregularities in the tubing.

It's my dad, I want to say. It's my dad. He's the one she's afraid of. He's the one she's been afraid of all these years and I brought him back into her life. He's the one. I'm the one. I'm the one.

I begin crying outside Mom's room and the policeman sees it.

"She's going to be all right," my father says, loudly enough for him to hear.

I am disappointed to see that Dylan's mom is the only one in the waiting room. I was hoping to see Dylan again.

"I thought I'd spend the night with her so you can both

rest." Mrs. Madsen is heartbreakingly kind and I can't stop crying. "Did something happen in there?" she asks me.

"It seems Charlotte had some kind of setback; the nurse is with her now," my father says.

"Oh dear, and she was doing so well just a little while ago." She pats my shoulder. "You need to get a good night's rest." She hands me some Kleenexes from the coffee table.

"Yes, she does," my father agrees. He digs his nails into my arm, which I take to mean that I should pull myself together.

I wipe my eyes. "I'm all right," I say.

He digs harder. I'm the bad daughter, obviously. What does he want from me? And then I know, so I say, "You don't need to stay, Mrs. Madsen, Daddy and I really want to be with her tonight."

He releases his grip on my arm. Now I'm the good daughter. Is this what he did with Mom? Good wife, bad wife? Pain is the way you know the difference.

"Are you sure?" For the first time I notice that Dylan has her smoky blue eyes.

"Yes," my father and I say together.

"You know, the police are finished with your house. I had some special cleanup people come over and do your kitchen. I don't know if you want to go back there, since they haven't found the killer yet, but with your father here, you might want—" She senses she may be taking liberties, probably from my father's disdainful gaze. "Anyway . . ."

I put my arms around her. "Thank you for everything," I say. "We couldn't have better neighbors." I hold her too long, probably. I wish I could go home with her. I wish I could have my life back.

"We're glad to help," she says. She picks up her bag from the sofa. "I'll be in touch tomorrow."

"Thank you," my father says.

She nods and heads for the elevator. I sit in a chair, but my father orders me like a dog, "Over here," patting the seat next to him on the couch. I sit down exactly where he tells me. When will this end? How will it end?

Except for us, the waiting room is empty. The television is set on a shopping channel. A woman is extolling the virtues of a new mop made of miracle fibers for just $19.95, and with that you get a free gallon of miracle cleaner as well. I pretend interest. I lean forward and cover my face with my hands.

"You've done very well so far," the demon father says.

When I don't acknowledge him, he twists my arm behind my back. I cry out.

His voice is a cold snarl: "You look at me when I'm talking to you. Do you hear me?"

"Yes." It comes out a whimper. "Yes. Please." I rub my shoulder when he lets go.

"Now, as I was saying—" His voice is smooth again. "You've done very well, and if you continue to do as I say you might end up being my daughter after all."

I shudder. What a thought. I want to cry again but I know he won't like that. It makes me sick to think of how I badgered Mom about him. What if she had told me the truth? Would I have believed her? Knowing the answer makes me feel foolish. Foolish, foolish girl.

Stop it, Red! Don't waste time blaming yourself. Wait for your opportunity. It will come. Be ready. Bella's voice is robust in my head. I sit a little taller.

Gail, the nurse, appears in the doorway and when she spots us, she walks over. "Her vital signs are still unstable. I've called the nurse-practitioner and the doctors, and they're all coming by to reassess her condition." She puts a hand on my shoulder. "It's going to take a while. Why don't you two go home? I'll call you as soon as I know anything."

I say what I think my father would want me to say. "No, we'll wait—"

"That's a good idea," he interrupts. "Thanks for your help. We'll be at the house. Do you have the number?" He stands up and waits for me.

Gail says she does, so my father and I leave the hospital and walk out into the warm spring night, Daddy holding my hand just as I've always wanted.

In the car, he makes me tape up my own ankles. I lay my head back and close my eyes. I am tired and hungry.

"Sit up straight," he orders, and I do.

It is dark now and the moon, which is almost full, shines above the dark shadows of trees and mountains. It's only a few minutes before we are on our street in Federal Heights. The first-floor lights in Dylan's house are all blazing.

Demon daddy pulls into the driveway and turns off the engine, looks up and down the street, and then opens the garage door with the remote control. He tells me to remove the tape from my ankles and while I do he moves around to my side of the car to let me out. Holding my arm, he guides me into the garage and then shuts the door. Sarah's car is beside Mom's and I am hyperaware that she is in the trunk.

"Can we let Sarah out of the trunk?" I ask. "She probably needs to go to the bathroom."

"She'll have to hold it, then," he says, and opens the door into the kitchen. When he turns on the light, I flinch. Even though it's spotless, the memory of the pools of blood, the splattered walls, is so fresh, I think I still see them. In fact, I look for bloody spots that might have been missed by the cleaning company but can find none. I stand with my back to the wall, waiting for him to tell me what to do. He takes the gun out of his jacket and holds it casually. "Why don't you fix something to eat," he says, motioning me over to the fridge.

I find sliced turkey and provolone and fix two sandwiches on two plates. When I'm done he tells me to sit at the table. "Sit tall," he says. "You slouch too much, just like your mother. Slouching makes you look disreputable."

I sit straight at the table and then he takes both sandwiches and sets them in front of himself. He pours himself a tall glass of Coke with ice and sits across from me, the gun on the table between us. Apparently, I have not earned a meal. I'm hungry, because Sarah and I never did have dinner and it's now after ten. I watch him eat and wonder if I am fast enough to grab the gun and shoot him. Is this my opportunity? Or is that precisely what he wants me to do? The gun scares me even when it's just lying there. I sit still and watch. My mouth is dry and the cold condensation on the outside of his glass makes me thirsty. I swallow. No sense in asking him for a drink. I'm being punished for some unknown offense.

He eats one sandwich and throws the other in the garbage. Half the Coke goes down the drain. It's a good punishment: I'm suffering, you bastard.

He pulls ice cream out of the freezer and spoons some out for himself.

The gun lies on the table. But if I pick it up, it might surprise me: It might be heavier than I thought, or clumsy to hold. Maybe it has some kind of release on the trigger that I don't know about. Maybe it's empty!

The doorbell rings. I look straight ahead and try to keep my face expressionless. Inside, though, there is a flicker of hope. He's the one who turns suddenly and slips the gun into his pocket. "Stay there, just as you are," he says. "Stay."

And I stay.

When the front door is opened, I hear Dylan's voice and my heart starts to pound. Is it because he might be able to save me? Or is it the danger?

"Hi," he says. "I saw the light and wanted to see how Mira's doing."

"She's doing fine," my father says, but his voice is cold. "We were just having ice cream. You can have some with us."

"Uh, no." Hesitation in Dylan's voice. "It's late."

"Oh, come on," my father insists. "You can watch the news with us."

"Well, just till the news is over." The door closes and pretty soon Dylan appears in the doorway and I'm so glad to see him, so glad not to be alone with the monster daddy, but afraid for him, for me, for all of us.

If I live to be a jillion and one, I will never forget the way Dylan's face lights up when he sees me, that nanosecond before he says, "Hey."

The gun comes down hard on his head. I let out a scream and Dylan grunts as he buckles to his knees and falls to the floor. He is not unconscious, but he is dazed and in pain.

I jump out of the chair. "Don't!" I cry.

My father, his foot on Dylan's back, the gun pointed at his head, hisses at me, "Sit. *Now!*" He presses down and Dylan winces. "I think this must be the boyfriend," my father says. "The one with the fancy play gun." He leans down. "This is a *real* gun with *real* bullets."

I sit at the table and cry silently, helplessly.

"Bring my briefcase over here." It leans against the wall next to the door leading into the garage. "Open it."

I do as he says.

"Take out the gloves in the pocket and put them on." They are men's gloves and are much too big, but I do as he says. "Now reach down in the main part of the case and pull out the wire."

At the mention of wire the hair on my neck stands on

end. I pull the wire out. It's a thin ring of barbed wire. "Tie his hands behind his back. Do it!"

I stand hunched above Dylan, crying. "Please," I beg. "Please just let us go."

The whack to the side of my head makes me stumble and the wire tears the flesh on my arm.

"Stop crying and do as you're told." His frenzy is building, and I realize I'm in hell and there's no exit.

You'll be all right, Mira. Stay alert. Bella again.

I kneel beside Dylan and wrap the wire around his wrists as loosely as possible, but the demon daddy cuffs me on the head and says, "Tight."

"I'm so sorry," I whisper. The barbs tear at Dylan's skin and he bleeds.

He squeezes his eyes shut.

"Go back to the table," Daddy says to me.

I take a few steps back and remove the gloves.

Daddy holds the gun in both hands and points it at Dylan's head. "Even if you hadn't come over so conveniently, I would have sought you out, Romeo boy." He kicks Dylan hard in the back.

I know he's going to shoot Dylan in front of me, and I hold my mouth with both hands to keep from howling.

"I would have preferred killing you slowly, but time is of the essence. We don't want your parents coming to look. We want to be gone from here." He bends and rests the nozzle of the gun in Dylan's ear.

He looks up at me briefly. "Say good-bye to your boyfriend, hon."

A noise stops everything. It's the garage door rising. Daddy swivels his head in the direction of the garage. Dylan is lying in front of the door to the garage, so Daddy turns and runs to the front door and opens it. I follow and can see Sarah running across the street to her house.

Now Mira, now! It's Bella's voice, and I know instantly what to do. With my whole body I shove against Daddy's back. He is thrust through the open doorway, stumbles and falls down the front steps. I grab Mom's flowerpots and throw them at him, aiming for his head. The thwack of one of the pots against his skull satisfies something deep in me. Daddy moans and flails one arm.

I rush back into the house, lock the front door, run into the kitchen, lock the door to the garage, and grab the phone and dial 911. "He's here!" I yell into the phone. "He killed my grandmother. He's out in front of my house. Come now. Hurry, hurry! Come right now!" I give the lady on the phone my address and she tells me to hold on until the police get there, but I hang up. I turn off the lights in the kitchen so the house is dark and crawl into the living room to look out the window. Daddy is dazed and lies on his side. I turned on the porch light so the police can see him plainly.

He calls, "Mira, Mira."

Go to hell, Daddy. I run to the kitchen and sit on the floor next to Dylan and begin removing the wire from his wrists. Sirens wail nearby.

"Where is he?" Dylan's voice is low and hoarse. He doesn't move.

"Outside," I say.

"Mira," Daddy calls more loudly, and now he's banging on the door. "Mira, let me in."

I hear the sirens on our street, the screeching of car brakes.

"Mira!" and then a shot through the door.

"Oh please, no," I say. "Please." I think he's shooting the lock on the door.

The door bursts open. Then there's another shot and even though I can't quite see it, I know that Daddy's dead, lying on the front hall floor. I know it, and I'm glad.

The police rush in, guns and flashlights in front of them. One of them turns on the light in the kitchen and I squint up at him. "Is he dead?" I ask.

"Yes, ma'am," he says. He bends down and looks at Dylan's head, which has a wet patch of blood where he was hit. "Call for an ambulance," the officer shouts to his partner.

Soon Ruth and Neal Madsen appear. When his dad bends over him, Dylan starts to cry. "You're going to be all right," his dad whispers to him. "It's over now. It's over."

"I have to call my mother," I say. "I have to let her know he's dead." There are people in the way. I can't get to the phone. "Please, I have to call my mother." I try to shove the police officers aside. The kitchen is crowded with them. One of them takes my arm and I shake it loose. "I have to call—"

Ruth Madsen clutches my face between her hands and says softly, "I'll call your mother on my cell. Look at me, Mira. I'll call your mother."

Her eyes are Dylan's eyes. I see it again. "He ran over the dog with his car!" I begin sobbing. "He strangled the dog and ran over it." Her arms go around me. I hold on to Ruth Madsen for dear life. "How's Sarah? Will Dylan be okay?"

A male voice comes from behind me. "We're going to need her for questioning."

Ruth grasps me tightly. "Not now. She's too upset." There's irritation in her voice.

"It has to be tonight while her memory is fresh—"

"Not now!" She is emphatic. She leads me to the sofa in Mom's study and we sit down together, still entwined. And without any feeling that I had ever left her embrace, I am lying on the sofa with my head in her lap and she is bent over me, stroking my hair and telling me that I will be all right. I shudder sobs at close intervals and then farther apart. I begin to anticipate having to talk to the detective and I begin to spin the story in my head. I elaborate on my vision of Daddy and of wanting to dance with him and paint with him, how we were tied by DNA, by the red hair and my grandmother with the red hair. How I dreamed of his elegance and culture, his gentility. I would speak of my disappointment and sorrow.

I cover my face. I was finding Daddy.

Chapter Eleven

Thursday

Sarah is the hero of the day. She is on the evening news telling how she pulled one hand through the handcuff, dislocating her thumb in the process. Her arm is in a sling, with a big bandaged thumb peeking out. "It took me about an hour and a half after I thought of it."

"But how were you able to get out of the trunk of your car?" Kelsey Chase, the newscaster, asks her.

Sarah, a large bruise on one side of her face, explains that in her car there are levers for releasing the seat from the inside of the trunk. "So you can put the seats down and carry stuff like skis or lumber."

Kelsey Chase says what an extraordinary teenager Sarah Sullivan is and how she helped to save the lives of two of her close friends, Mira Kent and Dylan Madsen, and to catch the murderer of local real estate broker Bella Kent.

Mom and I watch the news together from her new

room. Later in the afternoon she is taken off the respirator and made to walk with all the tubes and paraphernalia dangling behind her. She has a nurse on each side of her, and it's hard to tell if she's actually walking or if they're carrying her along between them. Mom is exhausted from the effort. We both sleep most of the afternoon.

Now I am sitting on her bed holding her bandaged hand and watching Sarah on TV. The follow-up to the story cautions parents to teach their children not to contact strangers on the Internet, even, as one newscaster said, if that stranger is a parent.

"I think they're talking about you and me," I say.

"Too little, too late." Mom's face too is swollen on one side and her smile is crooked.

I want to apologize again, but I know she will cry and say it is entirely her fault, so I resist. For now, we can't talk, except to blame ourselves.

Mom's room is a soft green, a perfect backdrop for the bouquets that take up every spare surface. Flowers from her teacher friends, the principal, and neighbors. My favorites are the pink lilies from Sarah's family. Exuberant lilies. Can you say that about flowers? They are on the windowsill, where Mom can see them without turning her head.

Sarah's parents appear in the doorway.

"Hi!" I say. "We just saw Sarah on television."

Both of them smile cryptically. "We won't be able to live with her after this. She's enjoying the publicity way too much," Dr. Sullivan says.

His wife moves to the bed and holds Mother's arm. "How are you? Are you in pain?"

"I'm on an epidural and can't feel a thing around my chest."

"Hurrah for epidurals," Mrs. Sullivan says. To me, she says, "Sarah's coming in a minute. She stopped off to see Dylan first."

"Oh, I'll go meet her. I went to see Dylan a little while ago but he was out for X-rays." I squeeze Mom's arm and head out the door.

In the hall, a woman studying a list stands in front of a caddy of hospital meals. The smell of cooked meat surrounds me. I am hungry, I realize, and stop at the vending machine for a candy bar, which I wolf down.

Dylan is sitting in bed, his head wrapped in gauze. Sarah, her hand still bandaged, sits in a chair at his side, and Joe sits on the arm of the chair.

"Hey," I say from the doorway. My voice catches a little. I'm aware that I'm the cause of all the injuries in the room.

"Hey yourself," Joe says. "Come in and join the beleaguered."

Dylan's smile is crooked.

"Did you see me?" Sarah asks.

Joe snorts and his voice rises in imitation: "Did you see me? Huh? Did you see me?" He blinks rapidly.

Sarah swats him. "Don't ruin my fifteen minutes of fame," she says.

"I did see you and you were wonderful. You saved our lives, you know. I mean you *really did* save our lives."

"Oh, she knows," Joe says. "Oh, how she knows."

I stand at the foot of Dylan's bed. "How are you doing?" I ask.

"I am glad to be alive," he says.

"Me too. It was a close call."

He nods. "Too close."

"That's what they all say," Joe says.

Sarah elbows Joe. "He has a skull fracture," she says.

"You do?" This is the first I've heard of it. "I thought you had a concussion."

"That too," Dylan says. "It's a hairline fracture."

"On his skull," Sarah says.

"I'm so sorry," I say. "I'm so sorry for everything I've done. Skull fracture." I chew the words in my mouth and blink back more tears.

"You couldn't know about him," Sarah says. "I'm sorry for you. I'm sorry it didn't turn out—"

"So your father really was Charles Manson," Joe says.

"Joe!" Sarah says.

Joe shrugs. "Well?"

I wipe my eyes with the side of my arm. "Some gene pool, huh?"

Dylan changes the subject. "My dad said your mother is out of the ICU."

"Yeah," I say. "She's going to be all right."

"That's good," he says. "That's really good."

"Where are you staying?" Sarah asks. "You're not living in the hospital, are you?"

"Actually, I am. Mom's room has an adjoining bath

with a shower and I packed some things after I talked to the detectives last night. I have my own little cot."

"You can stay with me—" Sarah begins.

"Thanks, but I really want to be with Mom right now." I turn back to Dylan. "When are you going home?"

"Probably tomorrow morning."

I nod. "Good." Awkward silence. What is there to say after the emotional calamity of yesterday?

"Okay, I have questions," Sarah says, flapping her good hand as if she's in class. "What I don't get is, how did your dad know where you lived? He can't know that from an e-mail, can he? I mean, the police reported this morning that he had killed Maude and stalked your house and attacked Bella and your mother, but how did he do it so quickly? You only found out how to reach him last Saturday night, and he's here on Sunday. I don't get it."

"Yeah—" I take a deep breath, delaying the answer.

"Caller ID." Dylan watches my face for verification.

I nod. "I called him, remember? I forgot about caller ID, because Mom doesn't carry it on her phone."

"And your last name would be on the caller ID," Sarah says.

I nod. "He told me exactly what he did. He bragged about it. He knew that Bella would be selling real estate. She's done it all her life."

"Wow," Joe says. "It was like he'd been waiting for you to call."

"Waiting to get even because we left him." I heave a sigh. "And I gave him the perfect opportunity."

Silence. "I'm sorry," I say. "I truly am." Silence again. We all have our heads down.

"Does this mean Sarah's not going to Europe this summer?" Dylan has his old smirk back. I grin with relief.

"Yeah, I think that's what it means," I say.

"Oh, damn," he says, and smiles.

"Oh, Sarah, I almost forgot! Your parents are up in Mom's room. I think they're expecting you to come in."

"I am, but I have to go get something out of the car." She stands, pushing Joe off the chair. "Come with me," she says to me. She turns to Joe, who is trying to stand out of her way. "Don't leave, I'll be back."

Joe raises his arms in surrender. "Yessir, ma'am. I'll just stay here with Master Dylan."

"Don't even—" She points an index finger at him.

He salutes her. "Yes, Mr. Sarah, sir." He turns to Dylan and says, "I think she has real bullets in that finger of hers. Big hunker bullets."

Dylan laughs a real laugh. It sounds good.

"See you," I say, and give a little wave. Sarah is already out the door.

"Good-bye, Kent girl," Dylan says.

I hear it, but I don't hear it. I mean, it doesn't compute immediately. Kent girl. In the doorway I turn and glance back at him. Our eyes meet and I get it instantly. He is breaking up with me. I am no longer Mira-me-deara. I am again Kent girl. One of the guys. I try to smile when I say it: "Good-bye, Madsen."

In the hallway a wave of sadness nearly chokes me. I

want to sob. Instead I swallow and swallow. Good-bye, Kent girl. Kent girl. Kent girl.

"Hey, the elevator's here," Sarah calls from down the hall.

Good-bye, Kent girl. I hurry.

Sarah's already in the elevator. I stand in front of her. "I'm feeling sick. Do you mind if I meet you in Mom's room?" I take my voice down to a whisper: "It's diarrhea." No one ever argues about diarrhea.

"Take your time," she says.

Good-bye, Kent girl.

I find a restroom around the corner and am relieved that all the stalls are empty. I go to the one farthest from the door and sit on the toilet without pulling my pants down. I take a handful of toilet paper and begin a silent howling into the soft tissue. Good-bye, Kent girl. I can hear his voice, see his face. Good-bye, darling Dylan. I wail into the toilet paper. I retch his name aloud: "Oh, Dylan," and I bawl good and hard, and when I'm done I think about Bella. "I'm sorry, Bella," and I start anew. I use up half a roll of toilet paper stifling sobs.

Someone enters and sits in the stall next to mine. She's wearing pink flip-flops. I sit quietly and wait for her to leave. When I hear the door close I get up and wash my splotchy face with cold water. I go back and sit on the toilet until I feel I can hide my sadness behind a more normal face. When I leave, the clock in the hall tells me a whole hour has gone by.

The Sullivans are gone when I reach Mom's room, and

she's sleeping. There is a lot of leftover dinner on her tray and I gladly eat the white roll with butter and some chicken. Mom's eaten the green Jell-O but that's about it.

The last of the day's light wanes at the window, shrouding the little room in darkness. I don't know what to do or where to go. I want to be unconscious. I pull back the blanket on my cot and find Daddy's book of pictures and watercolors. Sarah must have brought it from her car and hidden it there. I move it under the pillow. Wearing my clothes and shoes, I lie on the cot, pull the cotton blanket over my head, and fall asleep.

Chapter Twelve

Friday

The doctor wakes me when he comes on rounds. He is explaining to Mom how her lung was repaired and how it is now plastered against the lung cavity. "It should stay put," he says matter-of-factly. "Don't get in any car accidents, though." He allows himself a smile. It's a joke that isn't a joke.

I push my blanket away and Daddy's photograph album falls to the floor. The doctor stoops to pick it up. He looks at it briefly. "Someone's a good watercolorist," he says, handing it to me. "Did you do those?"

I shake my head and slip the book under the blanket.

"Any questions?" the doctor asks my mother.

"How long will I be in here?" Mom asks.

"Probably another week," he says. "Let's see how you're doing. I've ordered an X-ray for this afternoon. We'll see how your lung is doing then."

Mom has no more questions. The doctor pats her leg and says he'll see her tomorrow morning.

"He's cute," I say when he's left the room.

"He's married and he speaks with a royal 'we.' "

"Oh, Mom, stop being the grammar police." I turn the bed/chair into a chaise lounge and lie back, pulling the blanket up under my chin.

Mom smoothes her bedcovers. "He said, 'How are *we* this morning?' Well, I can't speak for him but I'm pretty good, considering." She looks at me. "Where did you get that photo album?"

I hate it when she makes this kind of switcheroo in conversation. I feel I'm being ambushed. "In the bottom of a drawer in Bella's desk."

Mom sighs. "Oh, Bella. Bella, darling." Her hand reaches out. "Let me see it," she says, and while I pull it out from under the blanket, she says, "She was supposed to throw it out."

I sit on her bed and hand the album to her. "I thought he would be nice. I thought that anyone who could paint like that would be nice." My head is on her shoulder as she leafs through the pictures.

"Painting may be the only nice thing he ever did," Mom says. "Oh, you look so adorable. That's why Bella couldn't part with this." She takes time with each photograph.

"Did you take the pictures?" I ask.

"Heavens no. He wouldn't trust me with such a project. No, he used a tripod and set a timer." She turns a page. "At first, he wanted you for himself, but when he perceived you as disobeying him—" She starts and turns directly to the last page of the album. Her breath catches in her throat and her hand goes up to her anguished mouth. "Oh," she says through her fingers. She closes the album.

"What?" I say. "What's going on there?"

She looks at me, eyes brimming, and shakes her head.

"Please," I say softly. "Tell me. Please."

I have to wait for her to compose herself.

"He broke your arm because you soiled your diaper when he thought you should be toilet trained. You *disobeyed*. He used that exact word." A gasp breaks through her lips. "He took this right after we got back from the emergency room."

I pick up the album and turn to the photo in the back. "He broke my arm?" It strains the imagination. My father smiling, smiling, smiling. "How old was I?" I touch the pink cast with my finger.

"Barely two," Mom whispers.

"Did you have him arrested?" I can hardly get my mind around someone breaking a baby's arm.

"I was too afraid of him. He said he'd kill you or Bella if I didn't do what he said." She wipes her eyes. "After this"—she looks down at the photo—"I began planning our disappearance with Bella." She blinks back tears. "I couldn't have done it without her. He never gave me any money."

I stare at the photo. "I'm glad he's dead," I say.

Mom's fingertips touch my hand. "So am I," she says. She clears her throat. "Why couldn't I see the psychopathology in him before we married?"

It is a rhetorical question, but I answer anyway: "Because he was charming and well-spoken and because he never needed the grammar police, I'll bet."

Mom smiles. "No, even in his most sadistic moments, he spoke perfect English."

We nuzzle.

"When we get home," Mom says, "I've hired a woman. I think you know her. The Sullivans use her as a housekeeper: Rhoda Bicknell."

"Sure, I know Rhoda. Are you hiring her for cleaning? I thought that was against your grand code of ethics." I change my voice to imitate her: "People should clean up after themselves."

She smiles and shakes her head. "She's going to be looking after me for the month after I get home."

"Mom," I say. "You don't need anyone to take care of you. I can do that. Really, I can. I want to." I want to make it up to her. I want to make her happy again.

Her eyes search mine. "Mira, I don't want you to have to take care of me. I want you to have a relaxed summer—be with your friends, do some reading."

"Mom!"

"The Sullivans are going to take you to Bear Lake for a week just after the Fourth of July."

"Mom, please—"

Her lips are pressed firmly together. She has already

made up her mind about this. "Mira, if I don't have some-one in the house, then I'll go to a convalescent home for a month. I don't want to place that kind of burden on you." She rubs my arm and kisses my hand. "I want you to learn how to drive. That's your job for the next month."

It makes me giggle to think of driving. "Oh, sure," I say.

"Oh, sure, nothing," Mom says. "I'm planning on giving you my Honda for your birthday."

I don't think I hear her right. "You're kidding." I can hardly breathe. "Aren't you?"

"No. I'm going to drive Bella's Mercedes."

"You hate the Mercedes," I say. "You told me you thought it was indulgent."

She bites her lip. "Not anymore. It was Bella's and I'm going to drive it." She pats my leg. "So that's it. I have spoken. I'll bet Dylan will be happy to teach you."

I release an unintended sigh and turn to look out the window. "Yeah, maybe." I don't think I'll ask Dylan. My father held a gun to his ear—*in* his ear—and was about to shoot him. I remind Dylan of that. And then too, I promised him he would be the one to take me to the air-port, and instead I had Sarah take me. I let Dylan down.

"What's that look?" Mom asks.

"Nothing," I say. And before she can press me, the or-derly interrupts with breakfast for both of us. Mom drinks some milk and takes a bite of toast but says she can eat no more. So I eat two breakfasts. It's barely enough.

I read *The Wind in the Willows* to Mom, who says it is

better medicine than anything else she can think of. Around ten-thirty Dylan comes in a wheelchair, pushed by a nurse. She stands in the doorway and he pushes himself into the room. He's wearing street clothes.

"How's the world's best English teacher doing?" He grins at my mom and high-fives her. She winces when their hands meet. "Ooh, the stitches are pulling." She smiles back at him. "But I'm on the mend. How about you? Are you getting out of here?"

"I am. My parents are waiting downstairs." His lips press together and he looks down at his lap as if he's looking for something to say. "So . . ."

"Your headache any better?" I ask.

He nods. "It really is. It's pretty manageable with painkillers." I get a brief smile.

"I'm glad you're alive, Dylan Madsen," Mom says. She reaches for his hand again and he gives it to her. "You were very brave."

He shakes his head. "No, I really wasn't at all brave." He nods at me. "Kent girl's the one who shoved him off the porch and threw flowerpots at him. I just lay on the floor."

I can't stand that he's calling me Kent girl. It's like a punch in the gut. I'll never get used to it. "Please don't call me Kent girl," I say before thinking. "Please don't. I'm Mira. Call me Mira."

I've shocked him. "Sorry." He clears his throat. He doesn't look at me and then finally he does look at me and now it's my turn to be surprised, because he's blinking back tears. "Mira." His voice breaks. He turns the wheelchair. "I've got to go. Get well, Mrs. Kent. Good-bye, Mira." And he pushes his way out of the room.

Mom's eyes narrow. "Did something just happen?"

I place *The Wind in the Willows* on her tabletop. "We broke up." I say. "I think we broke up."

"When?"

I shrug. "Yesterday, today." I blow my nose into a Kleenex.

Mom sighs. "He didn't look like he wanted to break up—"

"But he does," I say, not looking at her. "He definitely does."

"I don't understand how—"

She's interrupted by the X-ray technician wheeling in a portable machine. "Guess what?" He chortles. "It's X-ray time!"

I am blessed by interruptions.

In the afternoon, while Mom is napping, Sarah takes me to Hires to get a shake and fries and manages to make me laugh. She has taken off the sling and at every red light, she gives other drivers the thumbs-up sign with her big wrapped thumb. When we are drinking shakes in her car in the Hires parking lot, she says, "Your dad really turned out to be a—a . . ." She searches for the right word. "A crumb bum!"

"Crumb bum?" It's impossible to say without giggling. "You mean like a guy who eats crackers naked in bed, therefore making him a *crumb bum*?" And though it isn't *that* funny, I begin laughing.

Sarah tries to hide her smile. "Okay, I was trying to be nice about it. But he probably wasn't always such a nasty—"

I break into a guffaw. *Nasty* is suddenly the funniest word I've ever heard.

Sarah's expression is rueful. "Such a nasty toady." She snickers and I just fall apart. I try covering my mouth with my hands, but the laughter pushes out of me and so does some of the shake. I bend my head over the paper cup.

I take a deep breath. "It feels good to be silly," I say. "I thought we could never be silly again. I thought we would . . ." I look into Sarah's face.

"Die?" she asks. Her face is serious now.

"Yes, I thought that."

"I did too."

"I'm so sorry. I never should have contacted him."

"He fooled all of us," Sarah says. "He fooled me."

I don't really believe it. "You were skeptical to begin with," I say.

"Not so skeptical that I didn't go along," she says.

"I don't think he fooled Dylan. He was always suspicious."

Sarah takes my cup and places it on the tray in the

window. I hand her the sack of leftover fries. "I invited Joe and Dylan up to Bear Lake in July."

I know what she's going to say.

"But Dylan says he can't go—says he has to study for the SATs." She turns on the lights to signal to the carhop to get the tray. "Joe doesn't want to go if Dylan doesn't go." She turns on the ignition. "I guess it'll just be us girls."

Soon I will tell her that Dylan and I have broken up, but I don't want to explain how I know. She'd scoff and say I was imagining things, but I'm not imagining *Kent girl*.

Chapter Thirteen

June 18

It's my birthday and Sarah has made a cake and brings it over in the evening, singing "Sixteen Candles." We have it up in Mom's room, so she can join in the celebration. Rhoda Bicknell insists we have ice cream as well and goes to the kitchen to get some. Mom sits in bed, looking pretty good after all she's been through. Her face is no longer swollen; her bruises have turned a sick yellow. She has pain whenever she has to move from lying to sitting or from sitting to standing, but when she keeps still she feels fine. The cuts in her hands stiffen their movement, and she spends time every day trying to make her handwriting look normal. We have planned Bella's memorial service for the end of June. Mom has decided to take a leave from teaching and return to graduate school. We push forward.

After the singing and eating, I put on my bathing suit

and go swimming at Sarah's house. The air is warm and roses bloom profusely along one side of the yard. I think I smell them. After a few laps, we sit on the edge of the pool. That's when she asks, "Did you and Dylan break up?"

"Yes, I think we did," I say. I haven't seen Dylan since he left the hospital. "Why? Did he say something?"

"No, but Joe said that every time he tries to get a four-some together, Dylan doesn't want to go, and he didn't want to go to Bear Lake with us either."

"Then yes, we broke up." I laugh at her puzzled look. "We did it very"—I search for a word—"surreptitiously."

Sarah raises an eyebrow. "You've got to stop reading the dictionary," she says.

"I'm trying to catch up with you," I say. The sound of *Shrek* wafts through the open French doors. "How many times has your brother seen that movie?"

"A jillion, and you won't catch up with me. I'm much too smart." She digs me with an elbow. "So when did you break up?"

I throw a towel around my shoulders. "Since he called me 'Kent girl' at the hospital. He hasn't called me that since the Spring Fling. That's how I knew we were breaking up."

"That's it?"

I shrug. "I knew. It did the job."

"Geez, aren't you going to talk to each other?"

I shake my head. "I don't think Dylan wants to talk to me right now. I think what happened with my dad and all has gotten in the way."

Sarah looks down at the water and kicks it with one foot. "His dad called my dad to ask about a good therapist. He's worried about Dylan."

"Mom and I are going to therapy after Bella's memorial service," I say. "We still find it hard to talk about *him* and what happened to us."

Sarah laughs. "I'm going too. I wake up suddenly in the night with the most awful feeling of panic." Her eyes grow larger. "Like I'm in the trunk of a car."

A shadowy moon is rising above the trees into a darkening sky. "So he drove us all a little mad," I say. We both kick at the water.

"Yes, but we'll get better, and he won't." She is referring to my father. "He won't be back. Now if only we could make our minds believe that."

We sit quietly for several minutes. The crickets have started up, and I remember how slowly summer passed when we were very young, and I want to go back to those days—the days before Daddy—when Dylan Madsen was still my friend and Dr. Sullivan was my substitute father.

Later, when I'm dressing, I find Dylan's fortune in my pocket. It's been through the wash, but I can still make it out: "You will find love close by." I fold it back into my pocket. A few more washes and I won't be able to read it.

I know who I am. I am Pandora, who opened that box of woes and let them out into the human world. Before that, Pandora's life, like mine, was wrapped in shiny foil, reflecting friends and family. It was a gift. Her curiosity and her desire and maybe even her vanity led her to remove the lid from the box, and out it all came. It's the metaphor I live with nowadays. I let evil out. I killed Bella and Maude. I set it up. It's my fault. Don't even. I don't speak this aloud, because I know Mom would set out to make me feel better pronto. I don't want that. I know truth when it smacks me in the side of the head.

I tell this to Nancy Kooyman, my therapist, when we are alone. She tells me I have forgotten part of the story of Pandora, but I shake my head. I haven't forgotten.

"You forgot," she tells me, "that there was hope left in the bottom of that box." She leans forward and touches my arm. "Hope, Mira, hope."

Louise Plummer was born in the Netherlands and came to America with her parents when she was five years old. She grew up in Salt Lake City and received her BA and MA from the University of Minnesota. She recently retired as a professor of English at Brigham Young University. She and her husband, Tom, now live in New York City. She is the author of several young adult novels, including *The Unlikely Romance of Kate Bjorkman* and *A Dance for Three,* an American Library Association Best Book for Young Adults.

DEC   2007

AUG   7 2008